"We have a problem."

He looked up. "What problem is that?"

"You. . .we. . .we have to keep our hands off each other. I don't believe in it."

"You don't believe in letting a man touch your wrist?" He pulled the pie toward him.

"Not a strange man."

"Am I a stranger, Emily? Haven't I known you forever?"

She settled into her chair. "It feels like it, doesn't it? It's been a very strange day." She covered her face with her hands, then slid them so she could see him and still keep her burning cheeks covered. "I don't really know what to do with the ideas I have in my head. It's all new to me."

"Believe it or not, it's new to me, too."

"I don't believe it."

Jake shrugged. "All I know is there seems to be something inevitable about holding you."

MARY CONNEALY is an author, journalist, and teacher. She writes for three divisions of Barbour Publishing: Heartsong Presents, Barbour Trade Fiction, and Heartsong Presents Mysteries. Mary lives on a farm in Nebraska with her husband, Ivan. They have four daughters—Joslyn, Wendy, Shelly, and Katy—and one son-in-law, Aaron.

Books by Mary Connealy

HEARTSONG PRESENTS
HP744—Golden Days
HP818—Buffalo Gal

Clueless
Cowboy

Mary Connealy

Heartsong Presents

This book is dedicated to my husband, Ivan; not because he's a clueless cowboy, though—exactly the opposite. This is a book I wrote very early on in my writing life, and he was so kind about the time I spent writing and has been ever since. I would never have gotten a book published if he hadn't been such a good sport. It means so much when he says he's proud of me.

A note from the Author:
I love to hear from my readers! You may correspond with me by writing:

> **Mary Connealy**
> **Author Relations**
> **PO Box 721**
> **Uhrichsville, OH 44683**

ISBN 978-1-60260-264-9

CLUELESS COWBOY

Our mission is to publish and distribute inspirational products offering exceptional value and biblical encouragement to the masses.

PRINTED IN THE U.S.A.

one

Emily Johannson hadn't had a spare minute in a month.

Now, instead of a pleasant walk in the woods to unwind after spring planting, she was going to—she snagged a thick branch off the forest floor—run off some idiot.

A man tugged an ax from the bark of the magnificent tree in the Barretts' front yard. Muscles rippled under his sweat-soaked white T-shirt all the way to the narrow waistband of his blue jeans as he pulled the blade free. He hoisted the ax again.

Emily couldn't watch him hack away at that elm another second. She sprinted across the Barretts' lawn. Reaching him as his ax swung back, she grabbed the ax and jerked, throwing it wide.

The impact twisted him around, tipped him off balance, and dragged him over on top of her.

Emily's handy club flew as she fell. Her Stetson toppled off her head.

His roar would have knocked her down even if he hadn't fallen on her. His weight carried her flat onto her back and knocked a grunt out of her. The smell of a hard-working man and the ancient forest soaked into her head.

"Get off me." Her face, pressed against his chest, muffled the words.

He was already moving, but she gave him a good shove anyway. Sawdust scratched her fingers. His shirt was drenched and her hands slid up his arms and shoulders. For a split second she had her arms around his neck.

Furious brown eyes burned into her blue ones. . .then he rolled sideways and jumped to his feet.

Turning, he glared at her, his corded arms glistening with

5

sweat in the dappled sunlight.

She swallowed hard and tried to forget how nice he smelled. Oh yeah, the ax, her tree. She knew what she was doing again. She shoved the heels of her hands against the ground and stood.

"What are you doing on my property?" he snapped.

She heard anger in his voice as she dusted her backside. But his eyes spoke more of heartache and exhaustion. "*Your* property? The Barrett place is mine." It wasn't hers exactly, but close enough. "Who are you? And why are you hacking away at that beautiful elm tree?"

"How did you find me? Did Sid send you? Well, tell him to forget it." The man slashed his hand in the air. "I'm done."

"I don't know any Sid." Emily tucked her hands in the back pockets of her Wranglers, studying the varmint who'd invaded her home.

"Then I'll bet that real estate agent in Denver put you up to this. She's the only one who knew where I was." He ran a hand over whisker stubble and groaned. "A woman. . .of course a woman. Why can't I ever learn?"

"What are you talking about?" She raised her hands in the universal sign of surrender. "I don't know who you are."

He stared at her like a prairie rattler had turned up on his doorstep. Reaching for the blue denim shirt he'd shed when his slaughtering of innocent trees had gotten him too hot, he wiped his face with it.

Giving sweet reason a shot, she said, "My name is Emily." She nodded up the path she'd followed. "I live over the hill."

Raising his face from the shirt, his cheeks turned an amazing shade of red under what looked like two weeks' worth of scruffy beard. "How far over the hill?"

"A few hundred yards." Rats, she was going to have to lock her doors at night; the new neighbor was nuts.

"A few hundred yards? That's impossible. I was told there were no homes for ten miles. There are no other houses around here." He jerked his shirt on over his T-shirt so roughly she thought he'd tear the fabric. He stepped right up to her face. "I want some honest answers and I want them right now. How did you track me here?"

She knew she ought to be afraid—a complete stranger, remote location, no way to call for help—but she just couldn't work up a single shiver of fear for the poor guy. He looked exhausted and sad, thin...almost gaunt. He didn't stink or have the dissipated look of a drunk. No prison pallor. Not even an orange jumpsuit that said STATE PENITENTIARY on it. He just wasn't scary.

She had no trouble holding her ground. "Listen, hotshot. You're the one who doesn't belong here. Who are you and what makes you think you live here? And what kind of locoweed chops down an American elm tree?"

He looked up to heaven, as if praying and lodging a complaint at the same time. "I don't have to answer to anyone about that tree." He jabbed one finger toward heaven. "I own this land, and I can live any way I want. No one can stop me. And no one had better try."

As prayers go, Emily thought it needed work.

He glared at her. "I checked the plat maps. I talked to the real estate agent. You do *not* live a few hundred yards away."

"Barry Linscott told you no one lived out here?" Now Emily was mad. "Barry pulled a fast one to unload this white elephant on you? He hadn't oughta done that. The house is a wreck."

"Barry nothing, there was no Barry."

"There had to be a Barry. He's the only real estate agent in Custer County. We don't call him a real estate agent though. Too snooty. We call him the Guy That Sells Houses."

"I had a real estate agent out of Denver."

"That's right." Emily snapped her fingers. "You mentioned some woman you can't ever learn about. You were talking about her, right?"

"Look, lady—"

"It's Johannson."

His eyes sharpened. "Johannson is your name? That's weird. That's my name."

"Your name is Johannson? We're getting close. Any minute now I'm going to know who you are."

"My name isn't Johannson. It's Joe Hanson."

Dead silence fell over the two of them. Emily squirmed with impatience. Finally, she snapped. "What was the deal, hotshot? Did you get a whack and then the tree got a whack? My name's not Joe Hanson, it's *Johannson*."

"My name," he said through gritted teeth, "isn't Johannson. My name is *Joe* and my last name is *Hanson*. And my friends call me *Jake*. Please don't bother calling me *anything*."

That startled a grin out of Emily. Maybe he wasn't as stupid as she thought. "Joe Hanson and Johannson. That's kinda cute."

"Don't start monogramming pillowcases for us, sweetheart."

Her grin faded. "Don't flatter yourself. The only thing I'd monogram for you is a straitjacket."

Her new neighbor finished buttoning his shirt in grim silence.

"Why don't we talk about that tree?" She tipped an index finger toward the elm. That was the point of this, right? That and welcoming him to the neighborhood. She fought back a grin.

"What about the tree?"

"That's an American elm tree. You can't cut it down."

"We are surrounded by thousands of acres of trees. Are they all special or are your initials carved in this one?"

"Don't you know anything about trees?"

"Well, let's see. . ." He looked at the sky like he was thinking, then turned eyes the color of a chocolate Easter bunny—with rabies—back on Emily. "They burn well."

"Firewood?" Emily stormed up until their noses almost touched, even though he was about six inches taller than she was. She stood on her tiptoes and he accommodated her efforts to intimidate him by leaning down, vulturelike, to meet her. "You are cutting down this tree for firewood? *Are you out of your mind?*"

Jake took a step backward. "Let's start monogramming those straitjackets right now. I have a broom closet I can lock you in until the jacket's done. Or maybe you can just grab a broom and fly home."

"There is nowhere you can lock me"—she poked him in the chest—"and nowhere you can hide if you cut down that tree for firewood."

"Look, lady—"

"It is Emily. Emily Johannson. Stop calling me lady."

His jawed was clamped until his lips barely moved. "I won't call you lady. I'm not under any illusions that you are one. First you roll around on the ground with a total stranger—"

Emily's indignant gasp stopped him. "It wasn't *my* idea. You're the one who. . ." His expression hardened until the incredibly impolite things she wanted to say stuck in her throat. She sucked in a long breath. "I'm going to try and say one coherent sentence—one calm, rational sentence—'cuz, believe it or not, I'm a calm, rational person. I don't normally meet a stranger and start right in arguing. So let me say one sentence—"

"Just say it."

His interruption was so brusque Emily lost her train of thought. "Say what?"

"This sentence you're promising me. You've had three. You haven't said anything yet."

"Oh, okay, hotshot, here goes. Have you ever heard of Dutch elm disease?"

"That's it?" Jake's arms swung wide. "You get one sentence and that's it?"

"May I finish?" she asked with exaggerated politeness.

One corner of Jake's mouth twitched in what Emily thought might be a smile. "At least you're learning who's boss. By the way, why don't you drop the 'hotshot' while you're pretending to behave yourself? Finish your sentence."

"Answer my question."

"Question? Was there a question?" Jake ran one hand into his brown hair, sending wood chips flying. "The straightest line between two points is an impossibility with you, isn't it?"

"Dutch elm disease. Have you heard of it?"

"Yeah, I've heard of it—sort of."

Emily groaned and walked over to the elm tree to inspect the wound. "I should've known better than to ask a city boy. Dutch elm disease has killed nearly every American elm tree in this country. This old tree was planted by the Barretts' parents when they homesteaded in the 1860s. These trees started dying fifty years ago. My place, the Barretts', and the whole Black Hills lost millions of elm trees. It was a disaster."

Emily shook her head. "My parents and grandparents talked about all the trees standing dead, their branches naked and raining down for years all through the Custer State Park and the whole Black Hills National Forest that backs our land. For some reason this one survived. It's the only American elm tree left in these parts. It deserves better than to be hacked down by some Paul Bunyan wannabe for *firewood*." She noticed her Stetson on the ground, grabbed it, smacked it on her leg to knock off the dirt, and jammed it on her head.

"Look around you." Jake made a broad arc with one arm. "This place is lousy with trees. And I'm *not* going to burn it for firewood. I'm cutting it down because I'm planning to landscape the yard, and it's in my way."

Emily, in the middle of adjusting her hat, grabbed the brim so hard she almost ripped it off. "You'd destroy a majestic old tree because it's *in your way*?" Emily grabbed her stick, just to let him know she had one.

Jake glanced at the stout branch.

"Well, I say *it* was here first and you're in *its* way. How d'ya like that? And as for landscaping, this house is falling down around your ears. If you were stupid enough to buy the place, landscaping isn't even in the five-year *plan*. The flooring is all rotten, especially on the porch. And for heaven's sake, don't lean on any railings. They're just waiting for an excuse to collapse. The roof is shot. The bathrooms are forty years old and never worked that well to begin with. There are broken windows everywhere—"

"Look again."

After a moment to figure out what he'd said, she turned to really look at the house she had loved for so long. The roof was reshingled. The broken windows were securely boarded. The front steps were reinforced. He'd obviously spent a lot of time and money on it.

She turned back, confused. "When did you do all this?"

"I spent the last two weeks, working eighteen-hour days. How is it you've never shown your face until now?"

"You've been here for two weeks?" She knew even before he nodded with a single jerk of his chin that this work had taken that long. "It's spring. I've been working in the field from sunrise to after dark."

"Doing what?"

"Ranching."

"Ranching? You're a rancher? Do you have a family over that hill? Let me guess. Your cousin married you when you were twelve. You've got eight kids."

Emily laughed. How long had she been standing here fighting with him? Once she started taking bites out of him, she couldn't stop. The man was a living, breathing Lay's potato chip.

"My cousin?" she gasped the words out, laughing. "Eight kids?" She leaned against her precious elm tree, then straightened when Jake chuckled, too. From the rusty sound, she wondered how long it had been since he'd last done it.

"No cousin-husband then? No kids?" He sounded almost neighborly.

"No husband, cousin, or otherwise. I do have a kid. . .sort of."

The smiled dried off his face so fast Emily figured they were squaring off for round two. Or were they up to round five?

"How can you have a kid 'sort of'?" His lips formed a stiff, straight line.

"My sister lives with me. I dropped out of college and moved home when my mother died, to take care of my father and little sister. We've been alone since Dad died two years ago. Stephie is eight and she's at school right now." She saw him relax and wondered what other hornets' nests were waiting to be stirred.

With a start she looked up at the sky. The sun was getting lower. "I've got to be going. School's about out. I didn't reckon on having to save this tree when I set out for my walk. You know, now that I think of it, I have heard some sounds from this direction. I've been chalking them up to long hours and short sleep."

"Can you tell the time from looking at the sun?"

"Greenhorn." She rubbed her hand against the scarred trunk she was leaning on, looking down at the palm-sized chunk he'd hacked out of it. "Before I go, we've got to settle things about this tree. Your life really isn't worth a plugged nickel if you swing that ax again. I'll do you in, and if you're the loner you seem to be, no one'll ever miss you."

"I'm not a loner."

"Secrecy about buying this place. No local purchases. You're a regular hermit, Jake."

All trace of humor vanished. "Where did you hear all that?"

She'd hit another hornet's nest. "It's not what I've heard. . .it's what I *haven't* heard. If you'd so much as stepped into a store in Cold Creek, or even driven through town in that thing"—she tilted her head at Jake's shining black Jeep Cherokee—"I'd have known about it. Cold Creek is tiny. We notice strangers.

"You don't seem like the hiding-from-the-law type. I'd guess this is a back-to-nature kick or escape from your life. So, you're a hermit no one knows about 'cept me and that man-hungry real estate agent in Denver."

"Stop acting like you know me. You don't." His jaw clamped shut.

Emily grinned. "Now about this tree. . ."

He glanced at her club.

"If you take that stick, it won't save you. I'm bristling with weapons over yonder."

"The tree or my life, huh?"

She nodded. "Those are your choices, stranger."

He shook his head, sighing. "Would you believe that's the nicest offer I've had from a woman in a long time?"

"You think it nice of me to threaten to kill you?" He *was* loco. She hoped he didn't call her bluff 'cuz she didn't have any guns.

"No, I've just had some really nasty offers."

two

Emily didn't even want to think about that. "So the tree?"

"The tree lives." Jake offered her his hand.

She looked at it. "Is a handshake from a city boy playing lumberjack worth anything?"

His lips quirked into a smile.

She took his hand and looked at the sky again, anything but pay attention to his strong fingers surrounding hers. "I gotta go. Stephie'll be waiting."

She tried to pull away, but Jake held on until she looked at him. "Can you really tell the time from looking at the sun?"

Emily snorted and reclaimed her hand. "Straight up is noon. Dawn is at six and sunset is at eight. . .about. . .today. Add two minutes a day on each end till the first day of summer, then start subtracting. And don't forget daylight savings time." Emily was pretty much winging it. She'd checked the clock in her pickup truck before she'd come for this walk. But the sun told her time was passing. She turned toward the path. Just to be a brat, she held on to her stick.

She'd made it across the Barretts' yard when Jake caught up. "I agreed to spare the tree. You have to make me some promises."

She stopped. She didn't want this guy following her home. "Let's hear it."

"First, I want to see where you live. If you're lying and there's no house, I'm going to quit being so nice." He went on past her, toward the woods.

"You mean you can be less nice than this?"

Jake stopped suddenly at the foot of the trail. "This is so obvious it might as well have neon arrows. I can't believe I've never noticed it."

"Well, Daniel Boone is still king of the woodsmen." She jogged to catch up and politely tapped his arm with her stick. "About these promises, you aren't hiding from drug runners are you?"

Jake spared her a look of disgust. "Quit watching so much television."

Which wasn't really an answer. "Talk, hotshot. You asked for promises. Let's hear 'em."

He whirled around in front of her so suddenly she slammed against his chest. She looked into a pair of very annoyed eyes.

"I thought we agreed you'd quit calling me that."

"No-o-o." She shook her head. "Think back. We agreed you'd quit chopping down the tree. We never talked about *hotshot*."

"Keep it up, sweetheart. I could stand here and argue all day, and no one will be there to get your sister."

"No more hotshot?"

"No more."

"It really suits you."

He reached a jabbing finger toward her.

"Jake's fine. I can live with Jake."

"Good girl. Maybe you're trainable. I've been thinking of a collie, but you might do just as well."

He headed on toward her house.

"You know, Jake, ranching is a cold business. We bring baby calves into the world. We feed them, pet them, love them"— Emily's voice dropped low—"and then we eat them."

He shook his head and kept striding up the path.

She jogged even with him as they crested the hill.

He froze, staring at her old ranch house. "This is unbelievable. She'd said there were no houses for ten miles."

"Technically she's right. I do live ten miles from you."

Jake gave her a look that might have peeled her skin if she hadn't grown a thick hide since they'd met. "*You* may have escaped the cousin-husband thing, but they are thick like flies in your family tree, I'll bet."

"The road that leads to your driveway is a dead end. Everything west of you is in the Custer State Park. On the east is the Shaw ranch. He runs some cattle out here, but his fence line is at least a mile from you. He'd never come all the way into your place. Beyond that is the buffalo ranch he runs with his wife. So there are no houses forever that way. Plus he's got his cattle close up to his place right now because they're just done calving. You can walk to my place in two minutes, but on the road it's at least ten miles. To make it worse, they've got the old house site on the plat map on the south side of my land. I live in the new house."

"You have a new house?" He turned back to her obviously old house.

Emily laughed. "Sorry about that. No new house. My grandparents built this when my dad was three. They called it the new house, and I picked up the habit. Now about these promises?"

Jake rested his hands on his hips. "I don't want you to tell anyone I'm here."

"You *are* hiding from drug dealers." Emily lifted her stick. It felt like a solid oak security blanket.

He dropped his head back with a groan of impatience. "I'm not hiding from anything. I just want to be alone."

He tapped his index finger into her chest. "I don't want you to tell anyone I'm here. Should I say it again? Is it the cousin thing? Are you deaf? You didn't have any trouble hearing me chop your precious tree. Do I dare ask why?"

Jake folded his arms stubbornly. "Does it matter?"

"Beyond the fact that I'm dying of curiosity. . .no."

"Is there a chance you might really die of curiosity?"

Emily shook her head and wrinkled her nose at him.

Jake looked disgusted. "I never have that kind of luck. You look healthy as a dog."

She didn't miss his quick glance up and down her body, appraising her health.

"Get your hayseed expressions right. It's healthy as a horse."

"No, it's eat like a horse. Or is it a pig? Eat like a pig? That sounds familiar." Jake relaxed his stance enough to rub one hand absently over his stomach.

After one look, she forced her eyes up. "They both eat a lot. So do dogs."

"While we're on the subject of food, I don't suppose you have any."

Emily's heart turned over. With one thumb, she tipped the brim of her hat back. "You don't have any food?"

"I've got food," he growled. "I was just kidding."

He wasn't kidding, Emily could tell. "Come for supper. Does keeping you a secret include from Stephie?"

His fists clenched and his face darkened. "This is so familiar. I know *exactly* how women keep secrets. They all tell each other one at a time, swearing each other to secrecy. Pretty soon everyone knows and is laughing at the poor schmuck who trusted the first woman."

Emily shook her head. "Wow, how did you find that out? It's true, but I thought women were the only ones who knew it." She added darkly. "Some woman didn't keep the secret."

"Asking you to keep quiet is a joke, isn't it? Do you have any intention of respecting my wishes?"

"All right." Emily raised one hand as if she were being sworn-in to testify in court. "No one hears it from me. Not even Stephie. It's only a matter of time until she finds you herself. She spent most of the last two weekends at the neighbors' 'cuz I was busy, but the Barrett place has never been off limits."

"You let your little sister run wild in the woods? What kind of reckless behavior is that?"

Emily shrugged. "I did it when I was a kid. My dad did it before me. Until now, there's never been anything more dangerous here than a bumblebee."

"What do you mean, until now?"

"You're here."

"I'm not dangerous."

Emily couldn't explain it, but she knew without a doubt that was true.

"Just tell her to stay on her own property." Jake crossed his arms.

"Great, and how am I supposed to explain that without telling her about you?"

"See if you can't find the light switch for some of those unused rooms in your brain and figure it out. I bought ten miles of privacy." He looked skyward and jabbed his finger at the passing clouds. "That was the deal."

"You pray more strangely than anyone I've ever met."

"What difference does it make? He doesn't listen."

"Sure He does. Is that what you're out here for? To find God?"

"How about your sister?"

Emily gave up on evangelism. For now. "Stephie's going to find you. She'll be out of school for the summer soon, and I can't keep her away from your house."

Emily glanced at the sun again. "I've got to go, charming though this has been. I'll bring some food over later."

"Why would you feed me?"

She could see he couldn't comprehend her offer. "I always feed the new neighbors, and anyone within twenty-five miles counts. If you'd introduce yourself around, women would feed you." She could almost see the hair stand up on the back of his neck. "Nice, happily married women. People around here would be real good to you. Give them a chance. It might sweeten your disposition."

"What's wrong with my disposition?"

Emily couldn't help laughing. She turned away first for a change—that felt good.

"Why would you feed me?" he yelled after her.

Maybe no one had ever given him something with no strings attached. That idea made her want to be kind to him so badly she had to sass him to cover it up. "My intentions are honorable, hotshot. I'm fattening you up. You're way too skinny to interest any self-respecting carnivore."

She jumped in her old Dodge Ram, slamming the door. She looked back. Their eyes met and she couldn't look away.

With a little smirk, he touched one finger to his forehead and headed home.

ಭ

Sid Coltrain's search turned to destruction.

Jake had disappeared. He was running around loose. And if Jake started adding things up, Sid was in trouble. The company they'd started, Hanson and Coltrain, made a fortune. Jake led a team of engineers; Sid managed the money. Sid did his best to keep Jake too busy to get a close look at the books. He slammed both fists onto the desktop, then shoved the heavy piece of furniture. This remote log cabin was stark. The few pieces of furniture in the three-room cabin were as rustic as the building and heavy with dust—and a few footprints no doubt left by Jake.

Sid had finally tracked Jake here to Colorado. But Jake was long gone. Sid noticed the crumpled slip of paper under the desk. Smoothing it, he read *Cold Creek, South Dakota*, in Jake's bold, slashing handwriting. "Impossible," Sid muttered. "Jake hasn't stepped off a plane in the Midwest since the Tulsa tornado."

His voice in the empty mountain cabin mocked him. Reminding him there were no other leads. He pulled his cell phone out and punched 411. He hated talking to a computer, so he'd learned how to bypass them—no small trick. "Cold Creek, South Dakota," he snapped at the operator. "I don't know the area code. Look it up."

Sid seethed as he waited. "Operator, I'd like the number of... Jake Hanson."

No listing.

"Try J. Joe Hanson."

Nothing.

"Is there a Chamber of Commerce number in Cold Creek? Tourist information center?" Sid rapped his knuckles on the beveled corner of Jake's oak desk.

"A city office. . .a mayor's office? Well, what is there then?" Sid's only answer was a sharp click as the operator broke the connection. He snapped the phone shut. Jake wasn't in Chicago. Sid had people checking everywhere and this lodge in Aspen was the closest he'd come.

He looked again at the four words Jake had left behind. Everyone knew everyone in these small towns. Sid decided to put Tish on it. This whole mess was her fault. Jake would have never quit working if Tish hadn't messed up.

Sid knew he'd pushed his luck sending Jake to Honduras. He hadn't been home a week from the earthquake mess in Bolivia. But even an exhausted, burned-out engineer would have recognized the touchy financial situation at the office. Sid intended to put the money back soon, but for right now, he had some personal losses to cover. Sid couldn't let Jake hang around.

Whatever Tish had done sent Jake over the edge. No one had seen him for two months. Sid clenched his fist on the slender clue in his hand. Tish needed her boyfriend as much as Hanson and Coltrain needed its lead engineer. Jake was everyone's golden parachute.

Tish could take charge of this slender lead. He had to find Jake before Hanson and Coltrain collapsed around his ears.

Sid looked again at the note he'd found. South Dakota? Not in a million years! Jake employed a French chef and a chauffeur. Wherever Jake was, he lazed around in the lap of luxury.

№

He was pretty much living on Spam.

Jake knew how to rough it. That's pretty much all he did when he was on the job. But he was too burned out and depressed to even arrange the basics for himself. He'd driven into Cold Creek, seen what he was up against, and had driven back to

Rapid City, bought a trailer, filled it with building materials and canned goods, and come back to the ranch.

He'd gotten so sick of cold, canned meat he had to be starving before he could swallow it. He was close.

Soaked with sweat, filthy, every muscle in his body aching, Jake climbed down the ladder. He hadn't eaten since Spam at lunch. Under the grizzly stubble, his cheeks were sunken from the weight he'd lost.

He collapsed on the ground and leaned against the elm tree that had upset his neighbor so much. Truth was, it was a relief to let it live. Chopping down this huge tree was more work than he'd bargained for. He'd known after a couple of whacks he was going to forget the whole thing.

He thought about prickly, stick-toting Emily Johannson and grinned. Her hair—Jake closed his eyes and thought about that luscious, endless hair—her hair was like the forest, burnished oak, dark glowing walnut, and reddish chestnut glinting in the sun. And the blue of her eyes was as pure and honest as the wide South Dakota sky, while that soft cowgirl drawl eased into his bones.

None of that got to him like her sass, her courage, the warmth when she smiled, and the contagious way she laughed. She'd bring food. He instinctively knew she would.

Then he remembered Tish.

His instincts were garbage.

☙

Should she impress Jake with supper or slingshot him a pack of frozen hot dogs?

Emily weighed her options as she followed the winding gravel road on the six-mile drive from the lush valley Emily lived in to the clearing her neighbors owned. Beyond this rich, loamy, wooded area, the land spread out into the vast South Dakota Sandhills, with its sparse prairie grass, perfect for grazing cattle. The way was so familiar she could daydream full-time.

She pulled into the Murrays' drive. Stephie, swinging in their backyard, spotted her and jumped off the swing on its forward arch. Yelling, Stephie dashed toward Emily's pickup. Lila, the youngest of the Murrays' three kids, flew off the swing and ran over, too.

Helen poked her head out the door. "Come in for coffee."

"I can't, Helen. I'm way behind today."

Stout, dependable Helen—twenty years older than Emily but still a good friend—began striding toward the truck. Helen was firmly settled into the salt-and-pepper gray hair stage.

Emily remembered Jake's desire to be a secret, to avoid women, and Emily bit back a grin as she pictured Helen chasing after Jake. With a rolling pin maybe.

"If you're way behind, maybe you'll let short stuff stay the night." Helen ran a gentle hand over Stephie's light brown hair. Helen seemed as content with a dozen kids as with three. Nothing fazed her.

It would solve so many problems to leave Stephie. "She's been over here too much. I'm taking advantage of you."

Helen laughed and waved away Emily's protest. "You know they're less work when they're together."

Stephie clutched her hands together and started jumping up and down, begging. Lila Murray, Stephie's classmate, chimed in. Lila was a straggler in the Murray family, and she loved having someone her own age around.

Helen's gentle laugh rang through the riot. "We'd keep her all weekend if you said okay."

Emily held up her hands in surrender. "I give up. Do you need a toothbrush or pajamas?"

"We've got everything she could need. Are you sure you won't come in? Without this wild one around you might have some spare time."

"If I have to do her chores, I'm more behind than ever."

Stephie froze in her celebration. Her eyes widened with regret. "I'll come if you need me."

Emily regretted her teasing. Stephie's chores were simple.

Emily could do them in about five minutes, though they kept Stephie busy longer.

Emily stepped out of the truck and gave Stephie a big hug and kissed the top of her head. "I'll be fine, sweetie. I'll pick you up in the morning. And I'll leave time for coffee, okay, Helen?" She climbed back into the truck without looking Helen in the eye.

"I saw you going home around two thirty. Did something happen to keep you from unloading?"

Emily glanced at her groceries, still perched on the pickup seat. Emily kept her head turned to avoid the simple question. "I just got. . .uh. . .sidetracked." Emily waved without meeting Helen's eyes, called out, "Behave yourself, Stephanie!" and backed out of the lane.

Jake was safe for tonight. What would she make him for supper? She'd never thought of herself as lonely, but her reaction to Jake made her wonder.

She hit the gas.

three

She raced through her chores as if wolves were chasing her.

Not that she was eager to see Jake again or anything.

Then she made a meat loaf, scalloped potatoes, and a corn casserole. It was simple because everything went in the oven. She dug out of the deep freeze some sliced apples and a pie crust, knowing this was solely to impress him. She put the meat loaf in to bake, then added everything else except the pie. After a quick shower, she reached for her prettiest sundress. "Get a grip, Emily. This isn't a date. You barely know the man. . . and what you do know isn't good."

Emily forgot the dress and pulled blue jeans and a short-sleeved sweater out of the drawer. She drew a brush through her damp hair, then went and checked the oven, its door squeaking as the fragrant steam of cooking food escaped. In the gush of heat, Emily rearranged the casserole dishes to make room for the pie and slid it into place.

Then she forced herself to walk, not run, up the path.

&

Jake hadn't had more than a momentary flash of guilt in three hours. Way under his usual quota.

He was too busy thinking about Emily. He had to get her away from him, but before he did, he wanted one more taste of all that feminine kindness.

Despite his rudeness, he knew she'd show up with food. He listened for the padding of her feet and, when he heard her, he went into action.

Jake yelled, shoved the ladder leaned against the side of the house away from Emily's path, and then lay on the ground. She dashed around the house like he knew she would. He moaned and put a hand to his head and started to sit up.

She was kneeling by him in a second. "Oh, Jake, let me see if you're all right. Lay still."

Jake relaxed back on the dirt. He groaned, trying not to overact. Her hands smoothed over his arms and down his legs, checking for injuries. Contentment leached into his fully intact bones. How could such tenderness and grace be part of this prickly stranger?

She leaned over, her endless brown hair, unbraided, slipped over her shoulder and rained down onto his chest. His fingers itched to bury themselves in the silken length. She smelled so good—no perfume, just sunlight and fresh air and herself.

He opened his eyes and saw her fear. For him. Tears burned his eyes.

The last time he'd cried he was eight years old, the day he'd realized his mother had left for good. He'd cried one last time, then never again. No tears when he buried his father, none when he pulled tiny broken bodies out of mudslides, and he certainly wasn't going to start now.

"Did you land on your back? Did you hit your head?" Her hands flowed over him like warm rain. She caressed his forehead, brushed back his hair.

Her concern was too genuine, her touch too gentle. It awakened a need as real as thirst or hunger. A need he didn't know he had until now. A need so profound it scared him into action. He pushed her hands away and sat up.

"No, be careful. I think you might have lost consciousness for a minute." She pushed his shoulders back on the ground.

He found safety in hostility. "I'm fine. Back off."

She held him down. His eyes ran over the whipcord muscles in her slender arms.

"Don't fool around. You need to see a doctor. Lie still while I call an ambulance." She jumped up.

He grabbed her wrist and pulled her right back down on top of him. "Knock it off, Florence Nightingale." She'd have the whole state down on him in a minute. He'd have to prove he was all right. Time for Plan B: Send her running.

He dragged her head down and kissed her.

Emily jerked back and knelt on his chest. There was nothing soft and feminine about her knees.

She dug her kneecap into a rib and he let her go. She stood as he rolled onto one elbow and grinned. "I told you I was fine. The only thing you could offer me was that sweet sympathy."

Her faced flushed with anger. His plan was working.

"Come back here." He patted the ground beside him. Now she'd go away and stay away from the barbarian over the hill.

"Dinner's ready, hotshot."

"You're really feeding me?" Delight wiped all his planning from his mind. Then he remembered. "Where's your kid sister? Have you managed to keep our little secret for three whole hours?"

"My sister is staying with friends overnight."

Jake realized Emily had no survival skills to admit something like that to a complete stranger. He needed to teach her to be more careful. "She's gone all night? You arranged some time alone with old Jake? Good girl."

The rage on her face convinced him to stand up for his own safety.

"Do you want to eat or not?"

"I want to eat."

"I left it baking. If you have chores, you've got a few minutes before it's done. But I need to get back and turn the heat down on the pie." She started around the house.

He was beside her like a shot. "Pie? You made pie? You know how to make pie and tell the time from the sun?"

"That's right." She looked sideways at him. "I'm the last of my kind. You've stumbled on to Jurassic Ranch, hotshot."

He was starting to like his nickname. "So you made me a pie? You must really be hoping to impress me."

"If I want to make an impression on you, I'll use a hammer on your skull."

"I think I can smell it." He stepped up their pace as they walked under the canopy of trees on the wooded path.

"I've always figured perfume was wasted on men. The way they like hanging around in bars, I thought essence of beer and cigarettes was the way to go." Emily nodded like she was planning to go into business immediately.

"Are you trying to pick a scent to attract me?"

"Dream on." She walked faster. "I'm making a scientific observation. You're going to eat your dinner with the dog if you don't mind your manners."

"You know I'm having a wild thought."

"Not another one." Emily looked sideways at him.

"I'm thinking I might behave. Not because I believe you'd feed me in the dog dish. I've decided you're mostly hot air with these threats."

"Welcome to the party, Einstein. Your brain must've been runnin' wild all afternoon to figure that out." They crested the hill and headed across Emily's sloping lawn. "I didn't have much time to get ready for company." Her chin rose. "You'll take it as it is and like it. Our house isn't a showplace like the Barretts'."

"I think your memories are about twenty years old, honey. I've been living a life a caveman would pity the last two weeks. The old Barrett 'showplace' is a dump and it doesn't interest me at all right now. If the food I smell is for real, I'll gladly fight over it with the dog." He felt confident making the offer because there was no sign of a dog anywhere.

He pulled open the wooden door of the screened porch and held it open for her. She stepped past him onto the creaking wood floorboards painted brick red. Heading quickly to the inner wooden door, she shifted around so her back was pressed to the entrance, obviously reluctant to let him in.

He'd pretty much insulted her nonstop from the moment they'd met, and she hadn't paid much attention. From her expression, he suspected offending her home might be a mistake. Jake reached around her for the doorknob and she dodged away from his arm. He swung the door open and held it as she rushed ahead of him.

Jake stepped inside and his heart skipped a beat. The appliances were ten or twenty years old. The floor was beige linoleum trying to look like ceramic tile, roughed up in spots and curling in one corner. The walls were papered with faded yellow checks. The cupboards were fifty-year-old scarred oak, with little round white knobs, a couple of them missing. A round table with a white Formica top and tubular steel chairs upholstered with gold vinyl were against one wall of the small room, with a doorway on each side—one leading to the bathroom, another to a living room.

It was home. A real home. He'd never seen anything like it, and he loved it to the point of being speechless.

She moved quickly to the oven.

To cover his reaction to the house, Jake crossed his arms and leaned against the counter nearest the door, fighting a strong desire to move in.

To further his efforts to appear cool and collected, he said, "You've really got that happy homemaker bustle down. Where's the housedress? You need something in calico, floor length, and an apron made from flour sacks."

Emily checked whatever was in the oven. "Thanks. I thought I was acting more like June Cleaver, but you've backed me up a hundred years."

"June Cleaver, huh? Speaking of the Beave, how'd you arrange the privacy? Drop the munchkin along the road because you were desperate to be alone with me?" He had to tease her to keep from begging to stay. He breathed in the delicious aromas.

"Stephanie was invited to stay overnight at the neighbors."

"You shouldn't admit that to me."

"Why not?" She shut the stove and grabbed silverware, letting it clatter onto the table with no regard for her namesake, Emily Post.

"I'm a stranger. You just told me you're completely alone.

That's crazy." Jake had to focus to scold her. The aroma in the kitchen was enough to make him polite.

"Oh, sorry. Maybe if you wore a sign around your neck to remind me you're dangerous."

Jake shook his head. "You have no survival skills."

"Yeah, and which one of us is starving?"

She had him there.

"She's staying with Helen and Carl Murray. They are lovely people, and you should be so lucky as to someday have friends that nice." Emily set salt, pepper, and napkins on the table.

Maybe he'd been born suspicious. "You told her I'm here, didn't you?"

"Relax, I didn't say a word. I promised, remember? In South Dakota, that still means something. I agreed to it to protect you from Stephie for a little while longer."

"Can't you just tell her not to trespass? Don't you people know anything about private property?"

"Don't you know anything about living in the country? What are you planning to do, hide forever? Every little town around here will notice a newcomer. Will you drive to Rapid City every time you need milk?" Emily turned to the oven and jabbed a fork into something.

Jake wondered if she were pretending it was him.

Since Emily'd asked about his plans, however sarcastically, he decided to share his dream with her. "I'm going to live off the land." He couldn't control the pride and excitement. "I'm going to grow a garden and raise a cow and some chickens. I'm going to burn wood for fuel. I'll even make candles." His heart expanded with the longing to live close to nature. To experience health and clean air and simple food. He looked to her to share the beauty of it.

"Are you nuts?" She looked at him as if he'd grown a second head.

The woman had no vision. How far out in the wilderness did he have to go to find the true pioneer spirit?

"No electricity?" She pulled the meat loaf out and set it on a pot holder on the table.

Jake shook his head, waiting.

"No gas?"

"My mind's made up, and I'm hungry." He'd have been crankier if hot food hadn't been steaming in front of him.

"What have you been doing for food? No refrigerator? No stove? Are you cooking over an open fire? Eating canned stuff?"

He felt a flush climb his neck. "Well, I tried to build a fire. I did get one going. . .once. It takes an insane amount of time to collect firewood and light it and then, well, my cooking pan isn't right." He wanted to live off the land, not rough it by way of Cabela's and all their luxury camping equipment.

"Pan? One pan?"

There was that blasted compassion again. He wanted her to insult him so he could yell at her. Now that was fun. Instead she started that bustling thing again, all docile fifties' homemaker, putting hot casserole dishes on the table.

It smelled so good a wave of dizziness passed over him. He nearly collapsed into a chair. He wasn't starving, exactly, but he hadn't eaten anything good for two weeks. The food and her kindness drew him like a moth to a flame.

She slapped a plate in front of him so hard he looked up to see if she was angry. She spooned his food up without setting herself a place, like he was wasting away before her eyes.

Since she seemed worried, good manners demanded he put her mind at ease by eating. "What is all this? It smells fantastic."

"It's just plain food. Meat and potatoes and a vegetable. You must be starving if you think this is special." She piled corn beside the creamy slices of potato and a slab of steaming meat.

"It's fantastic food."

"You didn't eat this at home?" Emily scooped again for a bit, then sank onto the chair opposite him.

"Our housekeeper made. . .oh, I don't know. . .fancy stuff." Jake wished she'd stop shaking her head and staring at him like he was an extraterrestrial.

"Didn't your mother ever cook?"

"I didn't have a mother. And whatever housekeepers Dad hired were French chef types."

"No mother?"

He'd hoped he'd skimmed over that lightly enough, but she latched right on to it. "Look, I'm not going to discuss her. She's just another predatory female as far as I'm concerned."

He saw the questions in her eyes, but Emily was all mercy and restraint. She dropped the subject.

"Eat your supper. It was blazing hot from the oven, but it should be cool enough now." She injected a lighter tone. "If you've never had meat loaf before, you're going to die from pleasure, so say good-bye now."

four

Emily watched Jake take a cautious bite of meat. It looked like he was afraid it would bite him back.

She covered her dismay over his denial of his mother by serving up her own food, then watched the blissful expression on his face as he chewed in silence, and felt a surge of pride that he was enjoying her cooking. As he wolfed down his meal, she tried to get their relationship back where it belonged by being rude.

She set her spoon down with a sharp click. "I've finally figured it out."

Jake swallowed but, instead of speaking, put another forkful of meat loaf in his mouth.

"I know how to keep that mouth of yours quiet. I'll feed you. It'll cost a fortune, but the silence will be worth every penny."

Jake gulped down the last bit of food on his plate. Emily dished him seconds. He held his fork determinedly away. She could tell what it cost him.

"This is delicious. I didn't know how starved I was. But there's more to it than that. I feel like I've been hungry for this food all my life."

"Now do you believe I didn't follow you here?" While she had him softened up, she'd clear the air.

"No woman who can cook like this would ever have to chase a man. You must have a husband around here somewhere." Jake peeked under the table.

Emily laughed. "All women cook like this."

"I don't think I've ever even *seen* a woman cook. Our chef didn't like me watching." He started eating again.

Emily had been so fascinated by Jake's ecstatic reaction she'd forgotten her own meal. She took a few bites of a perfectly tasty meal that was nowhere near as interesting as Jake. "How can you live in a house without seeing where your food comes from?"

Jake just kept eating, apparently willing to let her say anything to him if he could have food.

"Have you ever had home-baked bread?"

Jake said, "No," around his potatoes, then swallowed. "You can bake bread?"

"You make it sound like cold fusion. How about ice cream, churned by hand?"

Jake shook his head.

"We try to make it a couple of times a summer." Emily smiled. "Feeding you's going to be fun. I hope you're this easy to please all the time?"

"Is this food really easy? Honestly, Emily, no fooling around. You didn't work on this all afternoon."

"Sorry if it deflates your ego, hotshot. I spent. . .maybe half an hour throwing this together."

"The pie, too?"

"Yep, but I had a crust and sliced apples in the freezer."

"Do you think you could teach me?"

Emily's own ego deflated. If she taught him she lost a perfect chance to make him her slave. "How am I going to give cooking lessons while you're hiding out from Stephie?"

Jake set his fork down with a clatter. "We've come full circle. What are we going to do?"

Emily missed his gushing compliments. "There's no way we are going to be able to keep Stephie in the dark."

Jake sighed. "This wasn't how it was supposed to be. I came out here to escape my old life. I'm no hotshot. I'm just a guy trying to slow down. If my business associate finds me, I'll be right back working hundred-hour weeks."

When he mentioned hundred-hour weeks, she suppressed a smile. She had just endured calving and spring planting.

She wondered what kind of easy life Jake pictured with no electricity and firewood to chop for heat. He was in for a rude awakening.

He picked up his fork and tapped it against his plate. "I'm going to die young if I don't make some changes."

All her amusement evaporated. "Is something wrong?"

He rubbed his hand across his mouth. Resting both forearms on the chipped Formica of her grandmother's table, he shook his head. "Nothing's wrong. I'm healthy. Surely you noticed I'm a nearly perfect male specimen."

Laughter surfaced from under her worry.

He chuckled, too.

Then she sobered as she thought of what he'd said. She looked into the rich chocolate brown of his eyes. "Seriously, what do you mean about dying young?"

His smile faded. "It's. . .well. . .my father died a year ago of a heart attack. He was fifty-six. We look alike. We act alike. He was a workaholic. I've spent the last year trying to slow down, but there seems to be only two speeds at Hanson and Coltrain—the speed of light or quit."

Hanson and Coltrain. She stored up this information about his identity. "So you're a workaholic, too?"

"If anything I'm worse than Dad. He at least took time to marry and have a son, though I'm sure I was an accident. . .or more likely a trap my mother set."

"Why a trap?"

Jake stared at his plate. "If she wanted me. . .why'd she leave me behind when she took off?"

Emily had no answer for the confusion and sorrow in his voice. She'd lost both her parents and knew that pain. But her folks had loved her and Stephie.

With a dismissive shake of his head, Jake went on. "I'm glad he managed to have a kid, even if he never spent a moment with me once I was here."

The derision twisted Emily's heart. "Well, life can't be so bad if you're glad you were born."

Jake glared. "What's that. . .cornpone wisdom?"

Now wasn't the time to get irritated just when he was talking about himself, but he sounded so superior. "I'd say it's just plain wisdom."

"I came out here to find a simple life. I wanted to get close to the soil. I didn't want anyone to know where I was because Sid will come charging in here from Chicago and wheedle me into going back. And I wasn't supposed to have to deal with neighbors." He looked furiously at her as if all his troubles could be blamed on her existence.

Sid. Chicago. Hanson and Coltrain. Jake Hanson and Sid Coltrain maybe? "The world is full of people, in case you haven't noticed. There is nowhere to really be alone. People aren't your enemy. Look in the mirror, hotshot. There's your enemy."

"I told you not to call me that." Jake stood with a fluid grace she tried not to admire.

Emily thought it was a shame his temper didn't scare her. Something needed to control her.

He rounded the table and she rose, backing away, retreating nearly to the living room before he caught her wrist.

"Let go of me."

Their eyes caught. The wounded man lured her. His hand tightened and he pulled her close. The timer went off.

His eyelashes fluttered. He released her and stepped away. Turning his back to her, he ran one hand through his hair, standing it wildly on end.

She hurried to the stove, snapped off the timer, and yanked open the oven door. She grabbed two pot holders and pulled out her bubbling apple pie, sliding in onto the stove top. She clicked the heat off, braced her hands on the countertop on either side of the stove, and tried to gather her scattered wits.

She breathed a quick prayer for some common sense. With unsteady hands, she cut the pie and set a slice in front of a subdued Jake, who had sunk back into his chair.

"We have a problem."

He looked up. "What problem is that?"

"You...we...we have to keep our hands off each other. I don't believe in it."

"You don't believe in letting a man touch your wrist?" He pulled the pie toward him.

"Not a strange man."

"Am I a stranger, Emily? Haven't I known you forever?"

She settled into her chair. "It feels like it, doesn't it? It's been a very strange day." She covered her face with her hands, then slid them so she could see him and still keep her burning cheeks covered. "I don't really know what to do with the ideas I have in my head. It's all new to me."

"Believe it or not, it's new to me, too."

"I don't believe it."

Jake shrugged. "All I know is there seems to be something inevitable about holding you."

Emily was stunned. "Jake, you don't even like women."

"You're right about that."

"We're just going to have to stay away from each other."

Jake looked down at the pie in front of him. "I'd die."

"From missing me?" Emily's heart started pounding.

"I was thinking about starvation."

And then she was laughing. She reached across the table and pulled the pie plate away from him before he could sink his fork in. "I know. I'll start trying to change you. That'll cool you off. And it'll be easy, too, 'cuz you're gonna hafta change."

Jake groaned.

"There, you're already irritated. Now I'll list off the things wrong with you."

"All right, you might be on to something here. Let's have it. Count off my faults. This is good. It's working. I already don't like you anymore." He raised his eyes to lock on hers. For an instant they flicked down to her lips. "Much."

Emily swallowed hard. "I didn't say faults exactly, just stuff you have to change."

"Let's just hear it."

"You have to get hooked up to electricity."

"No."

"Good, this is going great. You're really bugging me. No one lives without electricity if they don't have to. You'll figure it out soon enough, but get your stubborn pride and your male ego in the way so it'll be harder to back down. That way you'll suffer longer and blame me. That ought to keep you away from me." She nodded in satisfaction.

"I don't have a problem with my ego. And I'm not getting electricity. That's final."

"This is going great. Next, you have to have a new furnace. The house has an old one, but you need to tear it out and start over from scratch. That'll mean a bunch of workmen, so everyone will know you're here."

"No."

"Your idea of heating that whole house with firewood is ridiculous. It's got three floors and eight fireplaces. Do you know how much wood that will take? And it still won't be warm because chimneys make the house drafty."

"Barretts built it. They survived the cold."

"Yeah, but that's all they did. . .survive."

"How cold can it get in South Dakota anyway?"

The laugh that escaped Emily was pure derision. "I know you're not stupid, Jake. So why does stupidity keep coming out of your mouth?"

"Good one." Jake seemed to approve. "This is getting better all the time. I've got a forest full of wood, even without your pet American elm. I can live in the downstairs room with the main fireplace when it's cold and shut off the upper floors. If I hook up the gas and electric, the whole world will know I'm here. That's what you really want, isn't it? It's killing you not to gossip. Or do Helen and Goober Walton know all about me?"

Shoot, no amount of criticism was going to make her dislike him if she couldn't stop laughing. "Their names are Helen and Carl Murray, and I did *not* tell them about you. You won't even survive the summer. That's the real reason you need to stay away from me. Because you are playing Little Dope in the Big Woods, and you'll be out of here as soon as the novelty wears off. Wouldn't that be a nasty joke on you if the thrill was gone and you woke from your rustic pipe dream and found yourself with the girl next door clinging to you? A girl who has no intention of letting some burned-out house builder become important to her, while he runs around the world playing What Do I Want to Be When I Grow Up?"

"I'm an architect, not a house builder. An architectural engineer to be exact. They're long words but try to remember. I'm good at it, too. I'm not burned out, I'm simplifying my life. I'm planning to go to work again but on a smaller scale."

"Right, and I'm not a rancher. I'm in agribusiness and I do domestic engineering as a sideline. You're worried about dying young, but I've got a news flash for you. You're going to die before the summer's out. You'll poison yourself with spoiled food, or you'll hurt yourself and not have a phone to call 911."

"I won't—"

"And quit interrupting me. I've got a whole bunch more changes you need to make. We haven't even scratched the surface."

"I think I've heard enough. It's having the desired effect."

"Too bad if it's enough. We've skirted around it all night, but the truth is I'm going to have to tell Stephie about you. She will find you by the end of the week. I might be able to keep her away until then. But school is out Thursday. After that she'll be around all day every day."

"I don't want her over there."

"You can stop saying that because she *will* be over there."

Jake clenched his fists until his knuckles went white. He breathed several quick shallow breaths and then forced his hands open. "Is there a chance she'd be able to keep it a secret?"

She knew the question was a major concession. "Look, I'll ask her. But she's eight. She's an open, honest little girl."

"A woman, of course."

five

She should have been offended by the shot at women, but near as Emily could tell, Jake didn't like anyone, so it was hard to take it personally.

"She doesn't see other children too often in the summer. She goes to town with me for groceries and church, but I'll watch her. I can't make any promises. But I can promise you she's going to find out."

"I know I can't keep living here a secret. I thought I could, but I didn't understand the crowd situation."

This time she had to grin. There were forty people in twenty miles.

"Listen, I don't just want to hide on a whim. I really need to have some time before I deal with my old job. The last five years I've become a troubleshooter, working with natural and man-made disasters all over the world."

Emily decided to google Hanson and Coltrain later.

"My life is just crisis to crisis. My father's death was a wake-up call. I hadn't seen him for ages. He was a lawyer, lived right there in Chicago, but we had nothing to do with each other. I've been trying to cut back, but my partner won't let up. So I left. I disappeared. If they find me, they'll need me. Lives will be at stake. . .or homes, or the air, or water, or the whole blasted planet. I've never been able to figure out how to say no. If they show up here, I'll go with them."

"And you're afraid it will kill you?"

"I *know* it will kill me. But it's not so much that I'm afraid I'll die. It's that my father never did anything but work. I don't want to die without living."

She stopped herself from reaching for his hand.

"So I changed my life. I saw the picture of the Barrett place in a real estate office, and it touched a chord. The slopes on the roof and porches, the balconies on the upstairs windows. . . I love that house."

"The tower." She understood the appeal of the old house.

Jake smiled. "The picture seemed like a dream."

"Like a place where Rapunzel might be imprisoned."

Jake smiled. "You're really in love with the place. That's what you meant when you said, right at first, it was yours. I bought it for a song. How come you didn't buy it and fix it up?"

Emily shrugged. They were in accord again and that wasn't what they'd been going for. But she couldn't pretend she didn't adore that old house. "You know I've never given it a thought. My life just sort of happened to me. I didn't exactly choose it, although I'm sure things have worked out according to God's plan for me."

"God's plan?"

"Yes, I was full of my own ideas. You know. . .vet school, a career in the city."

"A veterinarian?"

"Yeah, that was the plan. I had two years of college when my mom's death pulled me home, and my dad's death held me. That's how God meant for it to be. Stephie and I love it here. After Dad died, I was more interested in stability for Stephie than fantasies about a romantic old heap."

"Romantic, huh?"

Emily shrugged at the impression that word, from Jake's mouth, made on her. "It's like a fairy-tale house."

"It's definitely unique."

"Great-grandma Barrett was rumored to be a German aristocrat. Somehow, during a time when this whole area was still barely settled, they built that house with all its elaborate flounces. I've hated to see it fall into disrepair. I suppose I could have saved it. Mom and Dad's life insurance left us pretty secure, but it would have been a waste for just Stephie and me.

I can't believe you want the job now that you've seen it. I would have thought the floors would have rotted through."

"It's a mess in places, but the foundation is solid." His smile was self-deprecating. "I responded to the picture and the isolation. And here I am. I'm going to chop wood and eat food cooked over an open fire, breathe clean air, and sleep at night. You can't imagine how bad I've been sleeping for years. But since I've been here, doing manual labor instead of wrangling in my head about load-bearing walls, and state-of-the-art earthquake management, and miles of government regulations, and..." He fell silent. His eyes dropped to his pie plate. Then he rubbed his whiskery face with one hand.

She didn't think he'd go on.

"And body counts," he whispered.

Her breathing stuttered.

He rubbed his open palm over his eyes as if he would wipe away his thoughts. "I've been sleeping hard for eight hours a night. It's wonderful. I like it and I want to stay. If Sid finds me, he'll manipulate me into leaving. That means no public documents like electric bills. What are we going to do?"

Emily smiled. "I have an answer that's so simple you're going to bite my head off."

"All your answers have that effect on me."

"I've noticed." She shrugged. "Learn to say no."

Jake shook his head, scowling. "Great. Thanks, you've saved my life."

"I have. You're just too stubborn to know it. Learn to say no." Emily softened her words with a smile. "Learn to laugh. Learn to cry. Enjoy being glad you were born."

"You call that simple; I call it impossible."

"Well, you know what they say. . . ."

"Sure, they say big boys don't cry."

Emily laughed. "That's big girls don't cry and that's not what I meant. They say women cry, men have heart attacks. Isn't that what you're running from? A heart attack?"

"Who says that?" Jake's eyes widened in horror.

"I can get you started. I've got something that will make you cry your eyes out."

Jake's eyes narrowed with suspicion.

She slid his pie back in front of him. "Hot apple pie. It's so delicious it will make you weep like a baby."

Jake started chuckling deep in his chest and reached for his fork.

"How much laughing do you do?"

"You've heard every note of the laughing I've done since my father died."

"Do you miss him? I know I miss my parents."

"I don't miss him. His death just gave me a wake-up call."

In a gesture she knew was pathetic, she tried to substitute food for a negligent father. "Would you like a second piece of pie? You didn't get much supper."

"Are you kidding? I was most of the way done with seconds when other...um...things got in the way." He looked chagrined. "Sorry, no more of that. We're doing pretty good, aren't we?"

"Yeah, pretty good." She cut him another piece of pie and got ice cream out of the refrigerator without asking if he wanted any. The man didn't seem to know anything about food anyway. She dropped a generous scoop of it on Jake's pie and set it in front of him.

"What about Stephie?" She hated to ask.

Jake shrugged. "Ask her to keep it secret. Maybe I can buy some practice time."

"Practice time?"

"Saying no." Jake sighed contentedly.

Emily didn't even bother to serve herself any pie. She was saving of all her strength for pushing her luck. "What about the electricity and gas?"

"No."

"There's plenty of roughing it you can do even with electricity."

"Sid will be on me in a minute. The man is a bulldog."

"Okay, how about I get the hookups in my name. I could tell them I'm running some cows on your pasture, and I need electricity and gas. I couldn't put a furnace in, but you can get by without that until winter."

"It's not how I want to do it, and if this pie wasn't so good I'd start fighting with you again."

"Just think about it. You can live like you are now if I feed you. The water works, doesn't it?"

"Yes, the windmill on the place keeps the supply tank full, and I've got lots of water and good pressure, but it's cold water, of course."

"You haven't had a hot shower in two weeks?"

"Well, the cold ones get you just as clean."

"But that well water is freezing cold."

Jake shivered. "Tell me about it." He went back to his pie.

six

She served herself a piece of pie just as the sound of a motor drew her attention.

"Someone's here." Jake shoved his chair back with a loud scrape and dashed into the other room. Emily ran after him.

He shoved open a window in the living room, unlatched the screen, swung one leg over the ledge, and ducked his head through the opening.

"No, Jake. Not that window. There's a. . ."

He dropped from sight. Snapping bush mixed with muffled cries of pain.

"Rosebush." She rushed to the window and saw him limp out of sight into the trees, hoping he remembered about the creek.

Her porch door slammed. "Emily, where are you?" Helen Murray's voice made her jump away from the window and hurry toward the kitchen. "Stephie got sick and wanted you."

With what she hoped was supreme calmness, Emily stepped into the kitchen and saw the table, obviously set for two.

"Did you have company for dinner?" Helen asked.

Emily glanced at the living room where Jake had escaped, realized how that would look to Helen, and turned back. She'd promised Jake.

"Uh. . ." Lying was a sin. "Uh. . ."

Helen might be a country woman born and bred, with no education past high school, but that didn't make her stupid. Her eyes followed the direction Emily's had a moment before, and Emily knew Helen was thinking something worse than the truth.

Stephie helped ease the situation. "I'm going to throw up."

Emily dashed after Stephie to the bathroom and began

rubbing her little sister's back as she emptied the contents from her stomach.

"Nick Thompson went home from school sick on Wednesday. I suppose it'll spread to all the kids." Helen, who'd followed the girls into the bathroom, was minding her own business even though it had to be killing her.

"All your kids will get it now. I'm sorry." Emily tried to make the apology cover everything.

"I've seen the flu before. I know better than to worry about it. Do you need anything before I go? A hand with the dishes?"

Emily kept her eyes fixed on Stephie, ignoring the hint. "I'm fine. We'll manage. Thanks for bringing her home." She soaked a cloth with cool water and bathed Stephie's warm face.

"Are you going to be all right, honey?" Helen asked with maternal gentleness.

"I'm fine," Stephie said.

"I guess," Emily answered at the same moment. Emily then realized Helen had been speaking to Stephie.

Then Helen, with a furrow between her eyes, patted Emily's shoulder. "If you need anything, I'm here."

Emily nodded. "Thanks. I appreciate that. More than you know. Good night."

"Good night. Hope you're feeling better tomorrow, Stephie." Helen turned away with no answers.

Emily gave her full attention to Stephie. "Let's get you to bed, honey. Do you feel awful?"

"No, I'm better since I threw up."

"Did you throw up at the Murrays', too?" Emily gritted her teeth, dreading the response. She started Stephie toward the bedroom.

"Just once."

"Did you make it to the bathroom?"

"Sort of."

Poor Helen.

Emily helped Stephie undress. "Climb into bed."

"I'm hot."

Emily slid a nightgown over her little sister's tangled hair. The fever wasn't dangerous, but it was enough to make a little girl miserable.

"I hurt."

"Do you think you can take some medicine?"

"I had some at Lila's. Please don't give me any more." Stephie started to cry and rolled close to Emily kneeling by the bed. "Stay with me."

Emily sighed and brushed the soft brown hair back from Stephie's flushed, tear-soaked face.

Emily spent the next two hours tending to Stephie. When her little sister finally dozed, Emily cleaned up the kitchen.

As Emily wiped the last surface, she came to the pile of mail she'd tossed there this afternoon. She picked it up in town once a week. There seemed to be an awful lot of it. She reached for the first envelope and tore it open.

> *Dear J.J.,*
>   *Darling, I love you. What you saw between me and the pool man was a moment of madness. You know there's never been anyone but you. Please give me another chance. I ache with an emptiness that only you can fill. You're the one I want to warm my. . .*

Emily jerked her head sideways and slapped the letter against her chest in a desperate effort to stop reading. This wasn't hers! She ignored the clamoring curiosity that urged her to read further and grabbed the envelope.

> *J. Joe Hanson*
> *Cold Creek, SD*

It was so close she just assumed. . . Stu Fielding, the postman, had just assumed. . . She snatched another letter.

J. Joe Hanson. Again. Not J. Johannson for John Johannson, her father. J. Joe Hanson. Jake!

She started a pile. There must be ten letters for him. Someone knew where Jake was. It meant she was coming. Emily had to warn him. Unless maybe the woman who had written this letter had broken his heart. Maybe he had turned his back on the world because she had rejected him. Maybe he'd forgive her when he saw this letter and leave without a backward glance. Maybe he'd been imagining her when he'd pulled Emily close.

She closed her eyes, surprised by the hurt. There was no rational reason to care what Jake thought.

She flipped a second envelope over and saw the return address.

Hanson and Coltrain
Chicago, IL

Stephie was the least of Jake's problems.

Emily shook her head. It was past midnight. Her day had started at five. A loud groan from Stephie and a cry for water interrupted her thoughts. She helped Stephie sip some water, then sank into a rocking chair near Stephie's bed and watched her sister settle into sleep.

Emily tiptoed to her room. She finally collapsed into bed in time to hear Stephie moaning. One last check on her sister, restless and vulnerable in her bed, and Emily slept.

Emily awakened at five like she did every morning. If she didn't get up, the cows would probably come into her bedroom and get her. She had done a half-day's work before Stephie stirred at nine. Stephie's flu was pure luck. Emily's guilt at the horrible thought didn't stop her from being relieved that she could keep her little sister indoors all day, maybe all weekend.

The only trouble was Stephie was feeling much better. She didn't want to stay indoors, and normally Emily wouldn't have made her. This time she stuck to it like a burr. She had to have more time before she tried to deal with Jake meeting

Stephie. If they could just get through this weekend. . .

Emily thought of the mail and knew her mental gymnastics were a waste of time. Jake's secret was out. She had to warn him.

Stephie fell asleep after a light meal at noon. It was the perfect time to run the mail over to Jake and watch that explosion. She waffled for a minute, fighting the desire to take him some dinner. It would be easy. She could make up a plate of leftovers from last night.

Why bother? He wouldn't eat once he saw the mail anyway. He'd be busy packing.

She reached the edge of the woods and couldn't stop herself from slipping behind the same tree that had concealed her yesterday. She needed to gather her wits. How could she possibly have reacted to him as strongly as she had?

To clear her head, she paused for a moment to look at the old Barrett place. Jake's work was already paying dividends, but there was a long way to go before the house regained its old majesty.

Three stories were covered with ornamental details in the best tradition of high Victorian architecture. A wide veranda wrapped around the entire house until it was cut off by a tower that anchored the front corner. Balustrades, anchored by posts every six feet, trimmed the veranda. A smaller copy of the balustrades surrounded balconies around each window on the upper floors. On the third floor, gables grew out of the central window on each side of the house.

She loved every ridiculous flourish on this house, but her favorite part was the circular tower. It was four stories at its highest point and topped by a cupola. The Barretts had treated her like their own grandchild and let her explore every inch of this old place. She touched two fingers to her forehead to pay homage to her very much invaded realm and stepped from behind the tree.

He wasn't outside. She'd have to knock on the door. It would be interesting to see what he had done with the place inside.

She glanced down at her clothes. For a moment she regretted her decision not to change out of her work clothes. The faded blue jeans and flannel work shirt with the sleeves rolled up were tacky. She had been determined not to make a single effort to look good.

She had succeeded.

The mail tucked under one arm, she squared her shoulders and marched up to the front door and knocked. She waited a minute and knocked again. No answer. She looked at his Jeep, parked right where it had been last night. She scanned the area around the house for any sign of him working on an outdoor project. Where could he be?

She wanted to drop the mail and run. But she couldn't leave it on the ground. She didn't have the nerve to do what she'd have done for the Murrays—step inside and leave it on the first clear surface. She pounded a third time.

The door flew open. She nearly stumbled into Jake. His face was red and his shoulders were heaving. At first she thought he'd run from somewhere to answer the door, then she saw he was furious.

"Get in here." He grabbed her arm and yanked her over the threshold.

"What do you think you're doing?"

The mail scattered all over his floor as he towed her into the kitchen. He dragged her around to face him. "I was planning to die alone before I asked *you* for help. But you're here now. Make yourself useful."

"What are you talking about? Let me go." She jerked her arm against his grip and he let go. Of course she was where he wanted her already. "Is this what passes for good manners in the big city?"

"No, this is about my back." He pointed a thumb over his shoulder. "You throwing me out a window into a rosebush last night."

"Me throwing you out? You jumped."

"And had my first rotten night's sleep since I moved to this God-forsaken place."

"God hasn't forsaken any place, pal. So quit complaining and speak English. I had a rotten night's sleep myself. Stephie got sick at the Murrays' last night. That's why Helen came over."

She whirled away to grab his mail, shove it down his throat, and make a grand exit.

seven

She didn't even get her back turned before he grabbed her wrist.

"Get your hands off me." Emily tugged hard against Jake's iron grip, and when that did no good, she shoved against his shoulder. He staggered backward with a groan of pain.

Emily froze. "I didn't mean to hit you so hard."

"Don't flatter yourself." He released her and turned around and lowered his blue denim shirt a few inches off his shoulders.

Emily gasped in horror. His back was covered with slivers and thorns. There were terrible scratches and one large raw gouge on the back of his shoulder, right where Emily had shoved him. "This happened last night?"

Jake tried to straighten his back and Emily could see how much each move cost him. "Brilliant deduction, Sherlock."

"Sit down. Let me help you. Your poor back. I'm so sorry." Emily pulled him toward a chair.

"Just fix it, will you?" His teeth were clenched and the words growled out.

"Sit still. This will take a while." Emily's stomach sank. "Do you have a first aid kit?"

"I don't have a bunch of fancy stuff around here. Just get the thorns out."

"How about a needle?"

"Why would I have a needle? My back-to-nature kick didn't include embroidery. Are you going to help me or not?"

Emily braced herself. "You're going to have to come to my house."

"Stephie's there."

"I can't get these stickers out without tweezers, and I can't

52

leave Stephie alone much longer."

"No." Jake ground the word out.

Convincing him was hopeless, so she blackmailed him instead. "Then I'm going to call an ambulance. You have to have them removed and you know it. Now will it be Stephie or the whole world?"

The silence was deafening. It stretched until she thought choosing was beyond him.

Through gritted teeth, he said, "Let's go."

Emily couldn't imagine how much pain he must be in to agree.

He stood, raising his shirt up gingerly. Stooped, he headed out the door.

Emily noticed the mail strewn across the floor. She picked it up and tucked it discreetly under her arm, deciding to delay the bad news.

Jake entered her house without waiting for her, turned a chair so he straddled it, and eased himself down.

Without speaking, Emily placed his mail on the kitchen counter and then rushed to the bathroom for her first aid kit, taking a second to check on Stephie. Then she faced the enormity of the task. She heaved a long sigh to settle her fluttering nerves and, tweezers in hand, started.

Jake flinched at the first touch of the cold metal, but he didn't speak. She worked on him in silence, systematically removing the slivers. The occasional hiss of indrawn breath was her only clue when she hurt him.

"There, that's the last of the slivers." She flexed her cramped fingers and prepared to start on the dozens of thorns.

"You're done?" Jake's voice was awash in relief.

"Oh no. I've done the slivers, but the thorns will take a long time. Maybe hours."

Jake's back stiffened. "Hours?"

"You can't see how awful it is. I'll work as fast as I can. I'm sorry I'm hurting you." Emily's voice broke.

"You're not crying are you?" His voice softened a little.

"No, of course not." She rubbed the back of one hand over her eyes. "I should have warned you about that window. I tried but I was too late. You don't really believe I wanted this to happen to you?"

"I suppose not." Jake's shoulders slumped. "I had a lot of time to work up a solid case against you. It's amazing all you can get mad about when you have hours to fume."

"I heard you hit the bush. I should have known you might need help. With Stephie sick I just never thought. I'm so sorry."

"Look, quit apologizing, okay? It's not your fault. It was an accident."

She worked in a more relaxed silence for a few minutes. "I can't reach your lower back. The kitchen table is sturdy." She moved the salt and pepper shakers to the stove.

He stood and looked at the table uncertainly.

"It's okay." She pulled it away from the wall and motioned for him to climb on. "Lie down."

He glanced at her once, then slid onto the table without a word.

Her hands trembled as she began. Her tweezers slipped sharply, and Jake couldn't control his gasp of pain. "I'm sorry."

"That's all right." Jake's voice was hoarse but calm and encouraging. "You're doing great."

She wished he'd yell at her. His gentle tone made her fingers tingle where they rested on his narrow waist, and the tingling spread to her hands and up her arms. She gripped the tweezers more firmly and tried to control her wayward emotions. She had to finish so she could get him out of here before—

"Hi, Jake."

They both gasped and turned their heads hard toward the sound of that little voice. Their reaction startled Stephie into backing up a step.

"J–Jake? You know Jake?" Emily couldn't believe her ears.

"So, you couldn't keep a secret for a whole day." Jake's voice was low and angry.

She looked down at him.

He had raised himself onto his right elbow and turned half-way around. His eyes bored into hers.

"I didn't tell her. Stephie, how did you know about Jake?" Emily turned back to her little sister and Jake did, too. A long silence settled over the room.

"Come here, Stephie. It's nice to meet you." Jake stretched a hand out to her and Stephie shyly stepped toward him. She reached out her own hand.

"Stephie, I asked you how you knew Jake?" Emily repeated sternly.

Stephie dropped her hand and looked wide-eyed at Emily.

Jake glared over his shoulder. "Don't be mean to her."

Mean to her?

"I'm not!"

Stephie took a step backward again.

Jake turned to the little girl. "I'm sorry Emily scared you. She isn't mad, just surprised."

Where on this earth had that sweet voice come from? He hadn't bothered to use it on her.

Stephie stepped toward Jake again, and this time, she gave him a confident smile, reached out her hand, and took his. She didn't shake. Instead, she held on and looked at him.

"How do you know who I am, Stephie?"

"You live at the Barrett place."

Jake and Emily exchanged another glance, and Emily shrugged her shoulders. "You mean you've known he was over there and didn't tell me, honey?"

Jake shot her another warning look, like he was ready to jump to Stephie's defense at any time.

"He's been there two weeks. I didn't tell you because he wanted to be a secret."

"What?" Emily and Jake echoed their amazement.

Stephie pulled back but Jake held on to her. Tugging on

Jake's hand, she asked, "Didn't you?"

Jake's voice, barely louder than a breath, just reached Emily's ears. "Finally, a woman who can keep a secret."

Then in a more normal volume, he answered, "Yes, I did. But how could you tell? And how did you know my name?"

Stephie shrugged. "It was on something in your car."

Emily raised her eyes to heaven. "You've been snooping around his car? You shouldn't have—"

"It's only natural she'd be curious," Jake interrupted.

Emily resisted the urge to stab him with the tweezers. At least the tingling had stopped in her fingers. Having Stephie in the room was going to make it possible for her to finish Jake's back. Then she could throw him into the rosebush again.

"It's okay to be curious?" Stephie could ask more questions than a prosecuting attorney.

"Sure it is, sweetheart," Jake said.

Sweetheart? Who was this guy and what had he done with the grouch who had come home with her?

"How'd you get the stickers in your back?"

Emily fumbled with some version of the truth. Would Jake want to admit he was here last night? Did he want Stephie—

"I fell."

Stephie nodded in complete and trusting sympathy.

Emily wanted to hear more about her little sister's sneaking. It had never occurred to Emily that Stephie shouldn't roam freely in the woods. The Barrett place was locked up and there wasn't much in the woods that could hurt her. And there were certainly no people around way out here. Or so Emily had thought.

"Tell us about how you found Jake."

Stephie would have impressed the CIA. She'd spied and sneaked around the Barrett house, inside and out.

"You can't go in that old house. It's not safe." Emily knew Stephie had always considered the woods her personal play-ground, but she had long been forbidden to go inside the rickety old house, locked or not. Emily had a pang of failure as a mother. She wasn't old enough herself to know what rules to make or how strict to be. And Stephie was so well behaved and she'd been through so much. Emily had the sudden realization that her little sister needed some discipline, and Emily had no practice at it.

Stephie pulled a chair away from the table just enough to plant herself inches from Jake.

Emily forced her attention back to her doctoring.

eight

Jake hadn't been around children much. Mainly in airplanes, where he firmly believed they should be kept in cages in the belly of the plane with the pets.

But this one was special. He rested his eyes on the miniature of Emily. Her hair was a tangle of brown waves, finer than Emily's but just as long. Her sleepy eyes were pure blue innocence.

If Emily scolded her one more time he'd—

"Are you going to stay here forever?" Stephie sounded hopeful. She wanted him to stay.

He wanted to tell her yes, but he remembered the pain of broken promises from his own childhood. "Right now I'm planning to. That's why I'm fixing the house."

"It looks great. I love the bathroom."

"You like it?" So what if she'd been inside his house without permission. She was just a child for heaven's sake.

"I haven't seen it since you went to town last Monday."

"Well, come over anytime. I still want to be a secret from everybody else, but you can visit."

Stephie grinned. "Why did you leave Chicago?"

Emily choked.

Jake wondered what all this little imp knew. He looked at Emily. He'd forgotten she was there. Hard considering she stabbed him in the back a dozen times a minute.

"You okay, Emily?" Stephie asked.

Jake arched an eyebrow and watched Emily bite back a grin.

"I'm okay."

Jake turned back to Stephie and started talking about his father's heart attack.

Stephie held his hand and talked about her own daddy.

Then Jake picked up the trail of his own story. "I just spent three months in Central America in the aftermath of a hurricane. Climbing around in those buildings we found. . ." Jake ran a hand over his face, remembering the injuries with so little hope of healing in that primitive area.

Emily kneaded his neck. He was talking to Stephie but Emily was the one who could imagine the details. As her hands worked on his knotted muscles he began, without changing his tone, to talk to her.

"The need was so great. I didn't bother with buildings. I just helped carry people. . .children. . ." He couldn't go on about what he'd seen. He didn't want anyone burdened with those horrors.

"It's so selfish to worry about my own exhaustion after all they'd suffered. But. . .I can't do it anymore."

Emily ran soothing hands across the nape of his neck and between his shoulder blades.

He reveled in the touch until he remembered. "I finally got home. The long-lost engineer. The conquering hero returns. And found my girlfriend in my apartment with—" He stopped, remembering Stephie.

Tish had been a companion. If Jake needed a date for some event while he was in town, he took Tish. They were friendly acquaintances, that was all. He knew Tish liked to brag to her friends that it was more, but Jake had no real interest in her, nor she in him. But to find her there, using his condo, the disrespect of it when he was ready to quit anyway, so burned out—

He clenched a fist and rested his chin on it. "So here I am ranching. What do you think, Stephie? Would a real country boy fall into a sticker patch?" Jake made a face at Stephie and she grinned.

"I've done all I can do." Emily patted his shoulder. "There will be some I've missed. I'll check again in a few days. I'm so sorry you got hurt last ni—"

"I'll stay away from those stickers," Jake said, cutting her off. No one had said anything about last night. "Thanks for taking care of me. I'd better get home."

"Do you want some cookies? Emily makes the best homemade chocolate chip cookies in the whole world."

He needed to get out of here. Emily's groan told him she was dismayed at the invitation. To be contrary, he accepted. Well, not just to be contrary. He hadn't eaten anything since last night. He climbed off the table, pulled his shirt on, and took the chair Stephie slid toward him. He straddled it to protect his back.

"Does he need Band-Aids, Emily?"

Jake smiled. "Band-Aids, the most prized of all medical treatments to an eight-year-old."

"No, the best thing for him—"

"I'd like a Band-Aid." Jake knew better than to grin when Emily's eyes narrowed at him, but he did it anyway.

Stephie pawed through the first aid kit.

Emily leaned two inches from his face. "It would take five hundred Band-Aids to cover those battered shoulders, hotshot."

Jake grinned as Emily's face flushed with anger. He couldn't remember ever being so entertained by a woman. He watched her steal a glance at Stephie and wondered what ego-bruising crack she wanted to make. He really wasn't in the mood for that. What he was in the mood for was a kiss from Em—

"Here they are. Do you want me to put them on?" Stephie wanted to help, not to mention play with the Band-Aids.

Jake couldn't say no.

The story of his life.

"Just put two on the big scratch on his neck, okay? The rest will heal better uncovered." Emily glared at him.

Stephie ducked behind his back to start fussing.

Jake was surrounded by the Johannson women's care even if the one in front did hiss from time to time. Nothing had ever felt so good.

He couldn't remember why he didn't like women.

&

Emily turned away and grabbed the cookie jar. She fished cookies out and grabbed a plastic sandwich bag out of a drawer and threw the cookies in. "Jake told me he has to go home now." She looked at him.

"No, not yet. Please stay." Stephie jumped up and down.

Emily saw the anger in Jake's eyes. "How about if you come home with me, Stephie?"

A tigress awoke in Emily. "No."

"Oh, please, Emily. Please, please, please. I won't stay long. I'll do all my chores and help—"

The litany of promises was lost on Emily. She knew exactly what Jake was doing. He was proving that there was no way Emily could keep Stephie away from him. And the more Emily stood in Stephie's way the more she'd drive them together. And the more completely shattered Stephie's heart would be when he left.

Emily dropped to one knee in front of Stephie. "Honey, Jake seems like a really nice guy. I'm sure he is." When he wasn't torturing her. "But he's a stranger. You learned about strangers in school. And we had a lesson about it in Sunday school, too."

"Jake's not a stranger."

Emily thought of how much Stephie had snooped around the poor man's house. Stephie probably know the man better than anyone. "Jake—"

"I wouldn't hurt her."

Emily looked away from Stephie, and the hurt in Jake's eyes brought her to her feet. "But this isn't about you, is it? It's about rules and being safe." Emily did her best to beg with her eyes. "Back me up."

Proving beyond Emily's ability to doubt that Jake *wasn't* dangerous, he turned to Stephie. "She's right about strangers. I know you feel like you know me, but you need to practice all the rules you've learned, so practice on me, okay? You stay here and I'll come and see you later, with your big sister here. I'll come for supper. That'd be great. I'm starving."

Stephie grudgingly agreed.

"You're always starving," Emily muttered. Wonderful. She felt like she'd adopted a stray dog. Wrong. Jake was going to be way more trouble.

"And later you and Emily can come over and have a tour." Jake smirked at her, then headed toward the door.

Which cornered Emily pretty neatly into having to spend even more time with him. Which reminded her of her tingling fingers and the fact that Jake had a life he couldn't say no to, that was bound to catch up with him at any time and he'd leave—breaking Stephie's heart in the process. So how did she keep him away from her?

She knew. "Don't forget your mail, Jake."

Jake looked over his shoulder, no doubt to toss a smart remark at her. Nothing came out.

Emily passed him and grabbed the letters off the kitchen counter.

He was right behind her. "What is this?"

Emily glanced at Stephie and enjoyed watching Jake keep the explosion inside. He rifled through the letters, muttering words Emily was glad neither she nor her little sister could hear.

nine

"Where did you get these?" Jake's strangled question made Stephie twist her fingers together nervously.

He saw a pang of remorse cross Emily's face. She was being ten different kinds of coward to dump this on him with Stephie as a witness.

Emily squared her shoulders. "Stephie, you know how Jake wanted to be a secret?"

Stephie nodded, looking between them.

"Well, these letters may mean someone knows he's here, and he's upset. Why don't you go outside while we decide what to do?"

Jake couldn't believe it. Here was Emily's chance to turn Stephie against him. About five well-chosen words from her and his temper would erupt, and Stephie would never trust him again. And Emily obviously didn't want Stephie trusting him. But she hadn't goaded him. She was too fair, too honest, too decent, too kind. Resentfully, he knew that made him the biggest jerk in the room. The better he knew Emily the more he couldn't stand her.

"Does this mean you have to leave?" Stephie whispered, catching hold of his fingertips.

Stephie Johannson was probably already the best friend he'd ever had. He dropped to one knee in front of Stephie. "I'm not going anywhere, sweetheart. Let me talk to Emily alone, okay?"

Stephie laid a butterfly-soft kiss on his cheek.

Tears stung his eyes. He rested a big hand, callused from touching destruction, against her baby soft hair. Considering the bad news he'd just been handed, he was remarkably at peace.

"I want you to stay." She threw her arms around his neck.

He gently wrapped his arms around her and drew strength from her. Jake let her go and stood up with a calm that surprised him. "Go on out now, please?"

Stephie nodded and ran outside.

"Where did you get these?" He shuffled through them.

"The mailman gave them to me when I was in town. My father's name was John. I still get things addressed to J. Johannson. These are to J. Joe Hanson. You know how addresses get messed up on junk mail. It seemed likely they were mine."

He flipped to the open one, fingered it as he read Tish's return address. "Did you read all of them?" It was obvious the rest were untouched. But Emily had read Tish's drivel. Since Tish wasn't here to blame, Emily seemed the natural choice.

"No, I didn't read them. I opened that one from someone named Tish. Is she—"

"She's none of your business." He pulled the letter out and compressed his lips. "You read this. You must have. No woman could resist."

"I said I didn't read it, and I didn't. Well, at least not all of it. As soon as I realized it wasn't for me, I stopped."

He kept reading, glancing up to try to catch Emily's reaction, embarrassed to think Emily had been subjected to this. None of this implied-romance garbage was true. All he was looking for was a reason she'd sent the letter to Cold Creek.

Tish had precious little to do with why he'd taken off. But she'd definitely been the last straw. He'd been away three months and barely thought of her. He'd come home overwhelmed, knowing he had to get out of Hanson and Coltrain. He'd walked into his own apartment and seen the woman who had his keys so she could water his plants, entwined with his pool man.

Jake had left his apartment with the clothes on his back. There wasn't even anything in his home he wanted to keep. No pictures, no scrapbooks, not even an old football trophy. He'd sent a note to Sid, saying he was through.

Taking every bit of cash he could scrape together out of several bank accounts—a considerable amount—he hit the road. He'd stopped at his cabin in the Rockies, and in the window of a Realtor's office in the nearest town, he'd seen the picture of the Barrett house, huge, impractical, isolated, and so cheap he should have known better. But he'd recognized home.

Home had turned out to be a white elephant in Cold Creek, South Dakota, that was trying to kill him. Isolation was a snoopy, argumentative woman who cooked like a dream and an angelic little girl who didn't want him to leave.

Emily broke into his whirling thoughts. "These letters are sent to the town. There is no box or route number. Somehow they got the name Cold Creek and they're taking a shot in the dark. I'll return them with a note in the open one, explaining about my name."

Jake couldn't gather his thoughts enough to respond.

"Look, if you want to call her up and beg for forgiveness, feel free to use my phone."

The thought of talking with Tish made him shudder. "Send them back. Sid'll be here sooner or later. I make him too much money. But maybe they'll learn they can get along without me in the meantime." Jake shoved the letters into Emily's hands. "What a mess. I'm tempted to pull up stakes and hide somewhere else."

He looked out the window in the kitchen door and saw Stephie running across the lawn.

"I'll try to make it sound good, Jake. And I'll tell the post office to return any new mail."

"No, I'd better see it."

"But why? Surely it would be better to—"

"Just bring it home and let me look through it before you return it."

"Listen, hotshot. I'm not your secretary. Don't—"

"You're the one who offered to help," Jake said, cutting her off. "Then the minute I want something, you start meddling."

She was a woman. She had manipulated him from the moment they met. About the tree. About the way he was living.

Emily's straight-forward differences of opinion and Tish's deviousness were just different sides of the same coin.

He glared at Emily. "Just do as I ask for once."

Emily sighed. "Fine."

Jake wanted to storm off, but of course he had to say one last thing. "What time's supper?"

❧

"Have you found him?" Tish stormed into Sid's office.

Her yellow spandex dress started low on top and ended high on the bottom. Her mass of blond curls swayed and bounced right along with the rest of her.

"No, I haven't found him," Sid snarled. At least she spared him that vapid help-me-big-strong-man voice. "Any response from those letters?"

"Yeah, look at this." Tish snapped a piece of paper out flat and dropped it on his desk. "What do you think?"

Sid scanned it.

"Should we send the PI?" Tish jiggled her wrist while he studied the letter.

The sound of her bracelets set Sid's teeth on edge. The polite Miss Johannson told him nothing. But that scrap of paper from Jake's lodge in Aspen had said Cold Creek. "Yeah, I'll get the agency on it."

Tish kept jingling until Sid grabbed her arm. "That racket is driving me crazy."

Tish narrowed her eyes, and he let her go. She wasn't someone he wanted mad. She knew too much about how short Hanson and Coltrain was on cash. Without Jake, half the engineers had quit. Sid hadn't slowed his spending, neither had Tish, who had been on the payroll since Sid had introduced her to Jake.

"We're in trouble if we don't find him soon. Sorry I grabbed you." Then, because apologizing made him choke, he added, "You never did tell me why Jake took off."

"Yeah, I did." Tish jingled her arm a couple of times, caught herself, and clenched her hands.

"No, you didn't."

"Sending him to another job was what did it." Tish slid a hand up to rest on one hip.

Sid knew she was probably right. But he hadn't had much choice. "I'll call the PI." Sid grabbed the phone.

❧

Jake had managed to stay underfoot at most meals. He'd been so kind to Stephie that Emily was very close to lifting the "stranger" label from the man.

Not that he wasn't dangerous. Watching him enjoy his food and dote on Stephie put Emily's heart in terrible danger.

After picking up the mail, Emily stopped in the feedstore for mineral blocks on her way to fetch Stephie and Lila Murray from their last day of school.

Men sat around a table, drinking coffee, and they called greetings to her.

She noticed Wyatt Shaw among them. "How's the buffalo business?"

The whole room erupted into laughter. Wyatt's former hostility to buffalo and his now being the proud owner of a herd of them was the source of a lot of good-natured teasing.

"Fine."

"Tell Buffy I'll see her in church on Sunday."

"She'll be there if the baby doesn't come first." Wyatt's love for his wife was enough to handle all of the teasing in the world.

Emily did her best not to envy her childhood friend his happiness. The men went back to their gossiping while she paid for her mineral.

Just as she stepped out of the building, someone said, "A guy came around my shop askin' for someone named Jake Hanson. Told him about Lizzie and Edgar Hanson, but he said this Jake is a young guy." The low-pitched voice slipped out the rapidly closing door.

Wyatt Shaw asked, "Fella driving a maroon Taurus? All rusted out?"

"Yeah, that's him. Hung around town all day. Said he. . ."

The door snapped shut. Emily reached to yank it back open. She stopped herself. How could she go back in? She'd draw attention to herself if she asked about the stranger. She forced herself to go to the truck. She had to warn Jake.

Emily whirled to jump in her truck and race home and almost ran over Buffy Shaw.

"Whoa, girl." Buffy, hugely pregnant and smiling, raised her hands to catch Emily before she plowed right over her friend.

"Hey, Buffy. I'm sorry. I didn't see you."

Laughing, Buffy gave her an awkward hug. "That is the nicest thing anyone's said to me in months. I'm so big satellites can see me."

"Hey, you're due pretty soon, aren't you?" Buffy had on a lightweight black tank top with a picture of a buffalo on the front and the words SHAW BUFFALO RANCH in a curve about the buffalo. Emily had seen plenty of the shirts around—the Shaws sold them out at the ranch and in the mini-mart in Cold Springs—but Emily had never seen a maternity version of the shirt before.

Groaning, Buffy shook her head. "I've got two months to go."

"Well, that's not long."

Buffy's eyes narrowed. "Only someone who isn't pregnant would say such an obscene thing."

"Sorry." Emily laughed. Then, because Jake was always in the forefront of her mind, Emily added, "I just heard Wyatt say something about a guy snooping around."

"Yeah, it was weird. He said he was a private detective. I don't think I've ever met one for real before, but he had ID. Wyatt checked. At first we thought he might be asking about your dad. He said Joe Hanson, and Wyatt misunderstood and thought he meant Johannson, you know."

"Yeah, I can imagine doing that."

All too well.

"Wyatt wasn't about to send some strange man out to your place, so once he was sure the guy wasn't looking for you, he didn't tell him any more. Did he show up at your place?"

"No. We're so far out we don't get any traffic, so I'd have noticed if he even drove by the place. When was this?"

"Maybe four days ago. I'm not sure. Don't you ever get lonely, living out that far?"

Not wanting to ask more and maybe raise Buffy's suspicions about why Emily was so interested, she let Buffy change the subject. "I'm used to it. Stephie's great company."

They talked about the buffalo for a few minutes. "Well, I've got to pick up Stephie and Lila, so I need to head out."

"It was great to see you. Come over for dinner after church sometime."

"I'd like that. I've been so busy with spring work I haven't been anywhere. Bye." Emily fretted about the private detective all the way to school.

Emily picked up Stephie and Lila. The two girls screamed and giggled, thrilled that summer vacation had begun. Emily dropped off Lila at home and backed out of the driveway before Helen could catch her. She still hadn't come up with a good explanation about Friday night.

Stephie hadn't told a soul about Jake. She loved having a secret.

"It's okay if you run over to Jake's and give him his mail, but you come right home."

"Em-i-ly," Stephie drew her name out into about six syllables. "Jake isn't a stranger anymore."

Emily nodded. She didn't know when to take the "stranger" label off the man. Emily didn't know the rules.

Stephie ran off to Jake's.

Emily headed to the barn to feed her steers.

ten

"Emi-leeeee!" Stephie came tearing over the hill only minutes after she'd left.

Emily dropped her scoop and ran. "Stephie, what?"

"Jake's hurt." Stephie skidded, wheeled around, and took off.

Emily sprinted to catch her. Stephie veered off the path and Emily followed, ducking branches Stephie sent slapping back.

Stephie dashed down a slope.

Emily lost her footing, sat down hard, and began sliding down the hill. Her jeans ripped. She clawed at the ground to stop, then scrambled to her feet and raced on after Stephie.

Stephie ran around a huge, felled cottonwood and dropped out of sight as if she'd fallen into a hole.

Emily rounded the tree and her heart twisted in terror. Jake was pinned under the massive trunk.

"You found her. Thanks, sweetheart." He was talking. His eyes were open. His face was sickly white. What kind of internal injuries might he have? "Emily, thank God you're here."

Frantically praying as she tried to figure out what to do, she knew an ambulance could never get back in here, but the EMTs could carry a stretcher. But the tree? How could they move it? She looked up the hill. She could get her tractor in there but she didn't have enough chain.

"I don't think I'm badly hurt. Just stuck." Jake spoke with a scratchy whisper.

"What happened?" She could see where he had attempted to dig with his left hand. He hadn't made much progress, but it was a good idea. If he really wasn't hurt, maybe she could dig him loose. She slid down beside him.

"The tree rolled while I was chopping it. I found a dead one.

70

To spare the American elm." He attempted a weak laugh, but it ended in a moan of pain.

The tree clung to the side of the hill, the top farther down than the roots. It had already moved once. If it started rolling, they'd be crushed.

Stephie. She had to get Stephie out of here. Stephie held Jake's left hand. Emily would have a fight on her hands if she tried to send Stephie away. She didn't have time for a fight.

Jake's right arm was pinned between the tree and his stomach. He lay in a little crevasse washed out by spring runoff. That was the only reason he was still alive.

"Jake, hang on. I'll see if I can. . ." She shut up and started digging. She needed just a bit larger depression. With her hands it would take a long time. Stephie saw Emily and imitated her. The tree quivered.

"Stop." Emily used a voice that gained absolute and immediate obedience. She didn't know where it came from.

Stephie looked up, terrified. Emily had to get Stephie out of here. Maybe she could stabilize the tree somehow.

"Stephie, I want you to go back to our house and get something for me."

Eager to help, Stephie jumped to her feet.

"I need a. . .get. . .do you know where I keep the shovel? You know, the one with the blue handle in the toolshed?

Stephie nodded. "I know where it is."

"Good girl. And a rope. There's one in the barn, but you'll have to—" The only one she could think of was knotted to an overhead door. Stephie couldn't get it. She'd have to go herself.

"How about the swing rope we took down and put in the basement last fall?"

Perfect. "That's exactly right. Get that and the shovel and bring them to me."

Stephie bent, gave Jake's hand a last squeeze, and ran.

Emily turned back to find Jake's eyes on her. Something cracked in her heart to see him so vulnerable.

"Tell me what happened." She put all her fear into digging.

"I was chopping firewood, planning to build a fire and cook some real food." Jake took a ragged breath. He twisted his head to watch her. "I stood on the trunk, hacking at a limb. It slid. I lost my footing and fell, and it pinned me. I tried to dig."

Emily's stomach turned when she pictured Jake falling in front of this massive tree. If he had landed just inches up or down the hill or if the tree had buried him under the gnarled roots hovering by their heads, he would be dead. "How long have you been here?"

"I've probably been here since two o'clock."

Two hours. She worked doggedly, ignoring the rocky soil scraping her hands, praying as she worked.

"I don't think anything is hurt. I can feel my legs. My toes wiggle."

"What happened to your voice?" She wiped a filthy hand across her brow as sweat stung her eyes.

"I yelled for help for a long time, hoping you'd hear me." Jake's head sank back onto the ground and his eyes fell shut.

Emily stopped pawing in the dirt and leaned over him. "Are you all right?" She rested a muddy hand on his forehead.

His eyes flickered open under her cool touch. "I'm all right. It's just. . . I'm resting."

Emily leaned close. "We're going to get you out of here. Now don't go fainting on me. I may need some help."

"What can I do?" He sounded hopeless.

Emily couldn't stand it. "You'll do whatever I tell you to do, hotshot. Just because you're useless as a lumberjack doesn't mean you can't help me haul your ragged backside out from under this tree."

Jake grabbed her wrist and pulled it off his forehead. "Ragged backside? Where'd a nice girl like you learn that kind of rough talk?" The little flash of spirit was encouraging.

Emily smiled, pulled her wrist free, and turned back to digging.

Stephie came dashing through the woods, yelling, "I found the shovel and rope!" Sticks hung from Stephie's tousled hair. She had nearly as much dirt on her face as Jake.

"Great, honey." Emily jumped up, took the rope, wrapped it around the tree, and knotted it. She tied it to the nearest live tree. The rope couldn't hold the weight of this tree for long, but it might give them the seconds they'd need.

Stephie knelt by Jake, holding his hand. Emily wanted Stephie away, but her little sister needed to help.

With the shovel, Emily moved dirt in earnest. Her arms ached from the hard work and tension.

At last she threw down the shovel. Reaching under the tree, she scraped out a Jake-sized trench. She ran around the tree and dug until she met the opening she'd made. "Okay, Stephie. I'm ready to work where you are now. Can you let me in there?"

Stephie backed away but hovered nearby.

"I want you up the hill. Do you see that wild plum tree up there? The one with the white flowers?"

"Yeah, but can't I help? I want to—"

Emily faced her little sister. "You can help Jake by doing as you're told. I'm ready to pull him out now and I need space. Now go." Emily didn't issue many orders.

Stephie went.

Emily called after her, "You know how to call 911, right?"

"Yeah, do you want me to go call?"

"No, not now. But if—" Emily's throat closed, she swallowed and finished, "If you need to, you call, and call the Murrays, too. They'll come running."

"How will I know if I need to?" Stephie sounded so scared.

Emily hated putting her though this. If this went badly, Stephie would see awful things. Emily quit thinking about it. "You'll know. Just go on up the hill, darlin'." Emily turned back to Jake.

Jake grabbed her ankle. "We both know this thing is barely clinging to the hill. I don't want you in the way if it rolls."

Emily glanced up to make sure Stephie couldn't hear. "We try my way, or I call for help."

"I'm not saying I know a better way. I'm looking at that trunk hanging over our heads and I'm telling you, if the moment comes and you have to make a choice, I want your word you'll get out of the way."

"What do you want me to say? I won't die for you?" She tried for sarcasm, but her voice trembled.

"That's right. It's real noble, but what about Stephie? She's had enough people die. If this tree starts to slide, get out. That rope will give you the time you need and no more."

"What are you guys doing?" Stephie took two steps toward them.

"Stay by the tree." Emily tried to keep the fear out of her voice. If she was killed, Stephie's closest family was a retired uncle in Phoenix.

She looked down at Jake. "We're going to do this. It's going to work. So stop talking about people dying."

Jake gripped her ankle with surprising strength. "Promise me. I won't let go until you do."

Something warm turned over in her. She *would* die for him.

He must have read her expression. "Say it, Emily. Promise."

Instead, she said, " 'Greater love has no one than this, that he lay down his life for his friends.' "

"That sounds perfect. So let me give up my life for you."

"I didn't mean that."

"Why does your saying apply to you but not me?"

"It's not a saying. It's in the Bible."

"I've seen so many people die." His painful grip on her ankle eased. "I've seen the pain it leaves behind. If something happened to me, it wouldn't even create a ripple in this world, but Stephie needs you."

"I'm not going to argue about whose life is more valuable."

"Promise. Please. If I came out of this alive and you didn't, it would kill me anyway."

She had to put his mind at ease. "I promise. I won't die for you, and you won't die. For me."

She held his gaze until he released her leg. "Let's do it."

Emily turned to the uphill side of the tree. "If I can get your arm loose. . ." She concentrated on pulling dirt from under Jake's back.

"It's pretty numb. It won't be much use to us."

She quit digging and braced both hands on his chest. "This might hurt."

"It's been that kind of day."

She pushed down. His arm slipped free. The tree inched sideways.

"Get out of here." Jake's voice was a barely human growl.

"Get out yourself, hotshot." She jumped over him and tugged him into the hollow she'd dug. The tree quivered and slid another inch.

Emily grabbed his shoulders and pulled. The moist forest soil helped Jake slide. The tree pivoted on the rope. Jake's knees came out. He got his feet loose.

Jake's prison vanished under the roots. The roots swung toward them. The tree paused, straining against the rope.

Then with a loud snap, the rope broke and the log rolled straight at them.

eleven

Emily grabbed Jake and dragged him to his feet.

The thick, uprooted tree trunk bore down on them.

She shouted, "Jump!"

Jake found the strength to obey.

Emily dived after him. Something slapped her face.

Jake and Emily landed in the dirt, side by side, and turned to watch the tree crush everything in its path. Then Jake pulled Emily close with his left arm. A small tornado hit.

Stephie.

"You did it," Stephie squealed.

Jake grabbed Stephie, pulled her onto his lap, and tickled her.

Emily sat up. Things started to go black, and she dropped back on the cool dirt so she wouldn't pass out.

She rolled her head sideways at Stephie's giggles, studying Jake. He favored his right arm, but it seemed to be working. Stephie jumped away from Jake, yelling in excitement, and Jake got to his feet slowly, but he made it.

When the black receded and Emily's vision cleared, she stood, leaned against a less malevolent tree, and watched as Jake and Stephie celebrated.

"Jake, I want to look at your arm. You may need a doctor."

"Boy, you start crying doctor every time there's the least little trouble."

Emily looked up sharply.

"Gotcha." Jake laughed, came over, and touched her neck. The humor faded from his eyes. "You're bleeding."

"I am?" She looked into the warmest expression she'd ever seen on his face. And that included the first time she'd fed him meat loaf.

"You saved my life, pure and simple. I am your slave for life. Thank you. And I'm so, so very sorry you are hurt." He pulled his hand away from her neck and there was blood on his muddy fingertips. With a shudder, he pulled her into his arms.

Stephie threw her arms around both of them, nearly knocking them down the hill.

Emily's panicky reaction eased in Jake's strong arms. When she felt steady, she pulled away. "Let's get on down to the house."

She pushed out of their little circle and stood for a minute to make sure her wobbly legs would support her before she headed down the hill.

Stephie's childish chatter and Jake's smooth, deep voice followed her. They walked past the dead tree, rolled halfway to the house, and she couldn't stop the tears that spilled down her face. She kept ahead of them so Stephie wouldn't see. Emily wiped the tears with her muddy hands as she shooed Jake toward the kitchen chair.

The old Barrett place, despite its new roof, looked the same inside as she remembered. She'd been in and out too fast the day she'd found Jake hurt to notice much. Dark oak cupboards, half of them with doors missing, lined the kitchen walls over a row of floor cabinets. A cracked porcelain sink, stained with rust, was the only fixture. No stove, no refrigerator. The floor was covered with ancient linoleum, swirled light tan under a coating of dirt.

There were a few cans and boxes in the cupboard, a loaf of bread lying on the countertop, and a half-empty case of Spam on the kitchen floor. She shuddered. "I suppose you don't have any first aid stuff yet?"

Jake studied her face, then shook his head.

Emily was too upset to scold. "You're going to have to shed that shirt, hotshot."

"Since you saved my life, I'll let you get away with that name. I'm starting to kind of like it." He tried to pull off his battered T-shirt, but his right hand wasn't cooperating. Finally he reached behind his neck with the left and pulled the whole thing over his head. He looked at the decimated piece of clothing, then tossed it at a cardboard box full of trash. "Country life is hard on clothes."

"Oh, Jake." A scrape dark with dried blood covered his right arm from shoulder to elbow, the skin raw. His chest was covered in abrasions. She struggled to control her tears.

"It looks worse than it is." Jake cradled his right arm.

Emily started scrubbing her hands in the ice cold water from the kitchen tap. "Steph, I'm going to need some things from our house. Run and get. . .get. . ." Emily stopped. There was so much. "Jake, can you make it over to our place?"

"I think I can." He didn't sound all that sure.

"Do you have any way to heat water?"

Jake tightened his lips and shook his head.

Determined not to nag, Emily said, "Stephie, fetch the thermos from under the sink, fill it with the hottest water. . ." As the mental list lengthened, she paused. "You know what? Why don't you stay here and mind Jake?"

Emily hoped it was all right to leave him. She flashed on him lying under that tree, afraid that image was going to haunt her for a long time. "While I'm gone, you get him a drink of water."

"Uh, maybe Stephie should go with you." Jake was trying too hard to support Emily.

"I think stranger-danger time is over. The only person you're dangerous to is yourself, Jake. When's the last time you ate?"

"I had a little breakfast."

"Nothing at dinner?" Emily clamped her mouth shut on the scolding.

"The tree fell about the time I'd have quit for lunch."

"I'll scrabble something together."

He smiled apologetically and shrugged his shoulders.

She saw him wince, then she headed home at a run. She came back, packed like a mule. A cooler full of food and ice in one hand, in her other she pulled Stephie's old little red wagon bearing a thermos of hot water, a first aid kit, a tiny camping stove, and the kerosene lantern they kept around in case of power outages.

She cleaned and bandaged his arm, then quickly put together a hamburger and bean concoction and set it on the stove her parents had used for camping trips. While supper bubbled on the little stove setting just outside the back door, she and Stephie cleaned the kitchen. Then she spooned up food for Jake and Stephie. Her own churning stomach wouldn't settle enough for her to eat.

"I'm feeling almost human again." Jake finished wolfing down his supper. "That was delicious."

"I think you'd better go to bed now."

"What kind of host goes to bed while he still has company?"

Emily was relieved at his flash of spirit. "We're going now. I have chores to do at home." She thought of the two hours of hard work awaiting her just to do the bare minimum. "We'll clear up the supper dishes. But you look done in. You need help getting upstairs?"

"I sleep downstairs. I tossed a mattress on the floor."

"No sheets?"

Jake snorted. "Women invented sheets. What are they for except to get dirty and feel guilty about because they aren't washed?"

If he had been at full strength she might have braced Jake about his rude attitude toward women. His exhaustion saved him. "So instead, your mattress gets dirty and it can't be washed."

"When it gets too dirty, maybe I'll put a sheet on it."

"Yuck. Fine, get into your grubby bed. You look done in, except for your mouth. That's still at full strength."

"Don't you like Jake?" Stephie twisted her hands together.

Emily regretted her shots at Jake even if he had them coming. "Of course I like him. If he wants to live like this, it's his call, but I like to give him a hard time."

"You sound mad." Stephie's brow crinkled with worry.

"He's ruining a perfectly good mattress, but I'm not really mad." She shot Jake a warning glance to back her up.

Jake made a comical face at Stephie. "You mean she can be worse than this?"

Stephie giggled.

Emily managed a smile. "Go to bed, Jake."

"I'd like to take a shower."

"You shouldn't. You should keep your shoulder dry."

"What about my poor mattress? I'll get it dirty." Jake grinned wickedly.

For a second their eyes locked and her heart seemed to slow as she looked into the tempting warmth of his hot fudge eyes. She forced herself to look away. "Let me remove the bandages. I'll replace them before you go to sleep. Don't slip in the shower."

"Aren't you afraid I'll faint?" His teasing brought her gaze back.

"I'll listen for a thud."

Jake laughed.

As he disappeared down the hallway, Emily turned to Stephie. "You want to surprise Jake?"

By the time Jake emerged from a long shower, Emily and Stephie had worked wonders. He walked into the room, wearing sweatpants and a blue robe. His right arm was out of its sleeve, cradled against his stomach. His hair was still dripping wet, like he hadn't been capable of drying it. He had dark circles under his eyes and his face was drawn with fatigue and pain.

"Get into bed, Jake. I want to make sure you're settled before we leave." She knew she sounded gruff.

Jake's eyes narrowed, his jaw clenched, and he glanced at Stephie. "You don't have to send me to bed like a child."

The urge to protect him was so strong she had to be rude to stop herself from holding him. "Just hurry up. I've still got hours of chores at home." Emily squeezed every possible drop of poor-overworked-me into her remark.

Jake repaid her with a long silence before he turned to his room. He stepped in the doorway, and Emily waited for his words of thanks for all her effort.

"Where'd that come from?"

"That old bed frame has been in the Barretts' upstairs bedroom for years." She was pretty proud of herself.

"I ran home for the sheets. And that's an old bedspread we don't use anymore." Stephie, vibrating with happiness, dashed between them as they stood at opposite ends of the short hallway.

"Thanks." His eyes flashed anger at Emily as he forced the word past his lips.

Stephie danced up and took hold of Jake's good arm. She pulled Jake down low enough to plant a kiss on his cheek. "I gave you my favorite sheets."

He turned to Stephie, and all his anger faded. "It looks wonderful. Thanks, honey."

How dare he be so gruff with her, then so kind to Stephie. "We're going. Do you need anything else?"

Stephie gave Jake a final grin and danced out the door, leaving them alone.

twelve

He stepped close and bent near, the words for Emily only. "You'd better be planning to come over and make my bed every day and do my laundry. I told you I didn't want any of this, and I'm tired of you nagging me every—"

"Listen, you ungrateful—"

The slap of a door reminded her they weren't the only ones here. She glared at him as she spoke to Stephie. "What happened to Jake's mail this afternoon?"

Stephie came running, looking worried. "I dropped it out by the tree."

"Can you go and get it, honey?" She saw Jake's expression and knew he had a few choice comments to make. Well, so did she.

"Sure, be right back."

Emily followed Stephie to the front door. Then when she was out of hearing distance, she turned on Jake, who had followed her, glowering. "How dare you ask me to do your laundry after what you put me through today?"

"What I put *you* through? I was the one under the tree. And don't change the subject. This isn't about the accident. It's about your meddling."

"Of course it's about the accident. What you call meddling is me trying to keep you from getting yourself *killed*. Any moron could see that tree wasn't safe. It was barely hanging on the side of that hill."

"That tree looked like it had been there for years. How was I supposed to know it was so unstable?"

Emily fought down her temper because she could see Jake was out on his feet. "We'll sort it out tomorrow. I'll take everything away I brought over. But for tonight, just get some rest."

Stephie came skipping into the house with a fistful of letters addressed to Jake. "Here's your mail, Jake." Her voice was so full of hope and sweetness, if that big ox yelled at her—

"That's great, Stephie. I'll see you."

How could he be so nice to Stephie when he'd just been snarling at her? "Let's go home, Stephie. Let Jake get some rest."

"Okay, good night."

"Good night. Thanks for everything." He sounded like Mr. Perky.

She glanced at the sun. It was after eight. She'd wasted a whole day keeping Jake Hanson in one piece. And she'd probably have to do it all over again tomorrow if he insisted on chopping wood.

Of course he'd try again. He had to have wood. She thought of all the trouble he could get into and made a decision.

ào

The crash almost knocked Jake out of bed.

The house shook. Earthquake safety measures flashed through his sleep-soaked brain. He was on his feet, dragging on his pants despite his agonized muscles. The crash was followed by a roar. He thought of dams breaking as he raced around the side of the house. It was the worst natural disaster he could imagine.

Emily.

Driving a tractor taller than the first story of his house. Dumping wood out of a huge shovel mounted on the front of the bellowing machine. She backed away from the side of the house, leaving behind a small mountain of wood. She stopped the rolling monster and, leaving its motor roaring, jumped down from the cab and marched over to him.

She jerked leather gloves off of her hands and tucked them behind her belt buckle. "I figured that would wake you up, Sleeping Beauty."

She yelled to be heard over the clamor of the diesel engine. "Now you've got enough wood to last until Christmas, supposing you live that long."

Emily had risked her life to save him. By way of thanks, he'd insulted her, yelled at her, and then thrown her out of his house. He'd given up trying to understand himself, deciding to apologize first thing this morning. He remembered that for about two seconds. "Take the wood yourself. I don't need your help."

"What's the matter, hotshot? Afraid you'll be contaminated by wood cut with a chain saw and a log splitter and hauled with one o' them new-fangled tractors?" She exaggerated her soft South Dakota drawl. Coated with sawdust and sweat, her shirt was soaking wet even though the morning was cool. She had to have been working for hours to do all of this. And she'd had chores left last night.

He tried to imagine how incensed she must be to have worked this hard just to put him in his place. "Did you work all morning so you'd have an excuse to insult me?"

"Leave the ranch work to people who know what they're doing. You want exercise, stack the wood. You oughta be able to handle that." She sounded so smug and superior.

"I'm not taking that wood. I'm not taking anything from you."

"And I'm not going to let Stephie find you like that again."

"You did this for Stephie, huh? I don't think so."

"Go back to sleep for a few more hours. I've been up since 5:00 a.m. Those are rancher hours."

"I stayed awake most of the night because my arm hurt. You've probably had more sleep than I have."

Her eyes lost their fire. She'd been spoiling for a fight, and he hadn't disappointed her. But there was her dratted compassion when he talked about pain.

"Is it bad?"

He loved that tone—the caretaker, the nurturer. No, he hated it when she went all soft and sweet. It was all manipulation. So why had he played on her sympathy? His irritation faded. Her gentle words drew his eyes to her lips.

"Jake, I. . ." The words seemed to catch in her throat.

"What, sweetheart? Tell me what you want."

She looked like she wanted to melt into him. "Have we ever been alone for ten seconds without fighting?"

"I don't think so." Looking at Emily, he knew she didn't just want his money and his status. She wanted the deepest part of him. And she wanted him to give with his eyes wide open. He hardened his heart.

It must have shown on his face because trust faded from her innocent gaze. He was responsible for that and it struck him as the worst sin he'd ever committed. He clenched his fists to keep from reaching for her.

She took two faltering steps backward, then turned and stumbled toward the tractor. She climbed on and drove away.

He watched her disappear around the grove of trees that separated their homes. And he was left safely alone.

thirteen

A week without a crisis.

Stephie was at Jake's all the time now. Emily had given up pretending he was dangerous to her little sister. He came over to eat at least once a day, and he and Emily were polite to each other for Stephie's sake.

He'd kept the camping stove. Stephie said he was eating better. Emily had never run her ranch and home so efficiently. She did her chores and started inventing new ones. Working hard kept her mind off her neighbor. Or at least it kept her *away* from her neighbor.

She'd never told him about the conversation she'd overheard in town and she wasn't going to. Jake knew his past was going to catch up to him sometime. What difference would it make when?

He was healing and he'd started planting a garden. How could that be dangerous?

Stephie finished her chores after lunch, then headed over to Jake's. Emily wiped pouring sweat off her forehead and took a long drink from her battered gallon-water jug, taking a break from scooping that last few bushels of corn out of an otherwise empty bin. She was sweltering but grateful for the work out of the direct sun. It had been blistering hot all day, unseasonable for early June.

"Emily, come quick!" Stephie came flying over the hill from Jake's.

Emily's stomach lurched.

"Something's wrong with Jake."

Emily grabbed the top of the small round door in the side of the bin and swung herself through the opening, nearly knocking her head off in her haste. She landed and started running.

Jake was on his hands and knees in the middle of his garden.

Emily knelt beside him. She noticed he was badly sunburned. From the look of the spaded ground, he'd dug up a huge garden bed.

Jake groaned and raised his head as if it weighed a hundred pounds.

"Stephie, run into Jake's house and get me a big glass of water." Emily helped steady him as she tried to stand. "We need to get you inside."

He nodded. Emily dragged him to his feet. His legs showed all the strength of cooked spaghetti. With Jake leaning heavily on Emily, they made it to the house just as Stephie came out with a dripping tumbler full of water.

Stephie pulled the screen door wide.

"Thanks," Emily said.

She glanced up at Jake and saw his throat work silently. Too dry to speak even the simplest words.

Stephie held out the glass of water, and Jake reached for it with shaking hands.

Emily helped guide it to his lips.

He sipped twice, took a deep breath, and then finished the water in one long drink. He managed a ragged, "Thanks."

"Let's get you into a cool bath."

He stumbled forward toward the bathroom. As they walked, Emily noticed the improvement in the house. Once the work necessary for survival was done, like the roof, Jake had turned his attention to the inside. Old carpet had been torn up, uncovering solid oak floors.

As they passed the open bedroom door, she saw Jake had kept the bed. He had brought furniture down from the attic that matched it—two chests of drawers and an end table. He had cleaned the whole set and polished it. They gave the room a lived-in look, and for the first time Emily wondered if he might stay.

Emily ran her hand across his brow. Hot and dry. Not good. Heat exhaustion. "Jake, when you're working in the sun and you stop sweating, it's a danger signal."

Jake reacted with such a small nod of his head Emily couldn't bear to lecture him further.

Emily guided him into the bathroom and twisted the cold water knob on the tub. She switched the shower head on. She wished it wasn't so cold, afraid it might be too much of a shock, but Jake didn't have any hot water to add to the cold. She helped him take his books off, then steadied him as he stepped over the rim and under the stream of ice cold water.

Jake yelped at the icy blast, then sank into the tub under the running water. Emily left the water on so he'd get good and soaked.

What if Stephie hadn't run over when she did? Emily looked up at her little sister. Her eyes were wide with fear. Her face was flushed red from her long run in the intense heat. As Stephie panted, trying to catch her breath, Emily worried she'd hyperventilate.

"Stephie, would you go to the kitchen and get Jake more water?" Emily felt stupid for asking, considering the gushing water soaking her as she bent over Jake, but she hoped Stephie's wild fear would ease if she could help.

Stephie grabbed at the glass on the sink.

"No hurry, Steph. Jake's fine."

Jake's head came up and worry creased his brow. "Stephie, I'm sorry I scared you. I promise I won't work in the heat like that again. I know better, but...but...it's June in South Dakota. I never considered it could be dangerous."

Stephie listened but didn't lose the frantic look.

He shrugged his crimson shoulders, and although he didn't let it show on his face, Emily knew each gesture tugged at his damaged skin. "I'm sorry I scared you. How about if I let Emily teach me all about ranching so I won't ever scare you again?"

Some of the panic faded from Stephie's eyes. "I'll get you some water if you want me to."

"I'd like that. Thanks."

Stephie hurried away.

Emily turned to Jake. He held her gaze for a split second before he let his whole body sag against the back of the tub. "I did it again. She's been my only friend. I hate that I scared her. I deserve anything you say, and I'm too weak to run. So I'll just sit quietly while you tear me apart."

Scolding him wasn't any use when he was all docile like this. She decided to give him a few minutes to regain his strength. She glanced around the bathroom for a washcloth. Of course there were none. The bathroom was remodeled though—new fixtures, new plumbing, new walls and flooring, the works. It was beautiful. Jake must have slipped out with his trailer and resupplied his building material.

Emily knelt on the bathroom floor by the tub. "Jake, you may be a rotten pioneer, but you're a great plumber and a talented carpenter. There's no chance you might forget about getting back to nature and just go with your strengths is there?"

His eyes widened with surprise. "Come on, don't compliment me. I want you to treat me like the worm I am. Let's have it, the whole sermon. Get it over with while I'm sitting down."

She hunted through a cabinet, found a towel, and brought it back to his side. The water was getting deep and she shut it off. She dunked the towel in and bathed Jake's neck and face. "Just relax and cool down for a while. And don't worry. I'm planning to yell long and hard as soon as I'm sure you're going to live." She smiled and he dug up a wobbly grin of his own from somewhere.

Stephie came back with the water glass.

Jake reached a dripping arm over Emily's head. The water trickled down her neck. The shocking cold startled a squeak out of her, and he grinned. He swallowed the water in three gulps and handed the glass back to Stephie.

She quickly offered to get more.

"I'm really starting to feel better, thank you."

"I'm glad." Stephie grinned.

Emily wondered how this love had sprung up between the two of them. Stephie's face was still beet red and dripping. Her flying braid straggled, sticking to her sweat-soaked cheeks and neck.

"Come here, Steph." Emily wrung the towel out and wiped it over Stephie's face. Stephie sighed. Emily wiped her own face with the chilly cloth. "That does feel nice."

Stephie nodded, her panic forgotten.

Emily's own stomach was still twisting over "almosts" and "what ifs." "Now, I want you to go into the living room and leave Jake and me alone for a while. Is that okay?"

"Sure. Are you going to start teaching him about ranching right now?"

Ah, the innocence of youth. "That's right. Jake and I are going to have a long talk." Emily wanted Stephie to be well clear of the "talk." No sense having any witnesses.

Stephie skipped away, her fears forgotten. Emily knew, as always, Stephie believed her big sister could fix anything.

One look at Jake told her he hadn't missed the tone. She admired his bravery as he braced himself.

❧

Jake wasn't going to win any fights with her as long as she had him dunked in a bathtub. It made him feel about two-years old.

He took a deep breath and started before she could. "I blew it. I hate myself for scaring Stephie. I'm the lowest slug on earth and I know better than to let myself get so dehydrated and burnt, but I've spent so much time working in the tropics that I didn't think about a South Dakota afternoon in early June being dangerous. So, I'm an idiot who thinks he's a hotshot. There, I beat you to it."

Emily sighed. "All I have to do is look at this house and

see you are a talented, intelligent, hard working man. You just don't know the first thing about living off the land. I'm sure I would be just as lost trying to read a blueprint or"—Emily looked around her and gestured with a wide swing of one dripping hand—"fixing up a bathroom like this. How can I tell you what to do when I have to stay away from you?" She looked back at Jake.

He knew this was the bottom line. They had to find a way to work together for Stephie's sake, if nothing else.

"Tell me what to do?" Her voice broke. "You know I told you to learn to cry, but truth be told, I don't do much of it myself, not since Dad died. Life is usually so easy. I can't stand finding you hurt again. What can I do to help you?"

Jake could have shriveled up and died from the hurt in her voice. He was prepared for a temper tantrum. That he could handle. "Aren't you going to yell at me? Come on. It will make you feel better."

She tried to smile. "Give me some time. I'll get around to it."

"I'm sure you will." They lapsed into silence.

As soon as he regained his first drop of energy, his awareness of Emily began to build. He didn't know how to stop it. He'd been attracted to her from the first moment he'd landed on top of her. Whatever was between them had some chemical element. They reacted when they got together. But maybe, just maybe, for the first time, he'd try to control himself. "You know what I think?" Jake removed the towel from her hand.

Emily let it go without a struggle. "Nope, but I'd like to."

Jake had the distinct impression she was starting to be bothered by their proximity, too. She sat back on the bathroom floor with her knees pulled up to her chest and her arms wrapped firmly around them.

"I think you should give me ranching lessons."

"The trouble with us working together is we end up—"

"I'm going to grow up. How does that sound? There's enough electricity between us to power this house with no help from wires, but I'm going to behave myself. I have realized by now that I don't have a clue about ranching. That's one of the reasons the house is improving so fast. I'm not doing anything else. I forced myself to go out and start spading up a spot for a garden this morning. I don't have any seeds, but I thought I could just get the dirt turned over and then maybe buy a book. Stephie made some suggestions about what to plant, but aside from corn and pumpkins, she's not really that much help."

Jake rinsed the towel over his face and around his neck and down each arm. His right arm was still scabbed over but it wasn't tender anymore. Only a few of the deepest scrapes remained on his chest. The sound of the cold trickling water helped restore his strength. And he recovered enough to feel like a dope sitting in the tub, wearing his jeans.

Emily filled his glass from the bathroom faucet and he gulped it down.

He lowered the glass and admitted, "I don't know how to get any food out of this land. I'm supposed to live off the land, but how? Where's the food?" He looked sideways at Emily, feeling as dumb as she kept telling him he was.

She remained silent, watching him.

"So say something. What am I supposed to eat, huh?"

She opened her mouth, then closed it again.

"What? Say it." Jake started to goad her, then thought the better of it in the new spirit of behaving like an adult.

"Okay, ummm, I'm trying to make myself offer to help you live off the land, but living off the land is hard work. And I'm going to have to do most of it at first."

fourteen

"No." Jake laid the soggy towel over his heart. "I promise I'll help. And how about if I help with your chores. . .at 5:00 a.m.? Then you won't be doing that much extra."

Emily's snort made him want to sink under the water.

Instead he sat up straighter and wrung out the entire towel over his head. As soon as the water stopped flowing and his annoyance faded, he got back to the subject at hand. "What exactly am I supposed to do that's so much work? Explain it."

Emily sighed deeply. "Well, you need to grow your own vegetables and meat. You need a milk cow. You'll need chickens for meat and eggs. It's too late to plant most of the quick-growing garden food. Peas and onions and potatoes go in early. We're already eating those at our place."

"Yeah, I know. They're delicious."

"We'll keep sharing our spring garden with you and let you plant pumpkins and tomatoes and sweet corn over here for us."

"Chickens and a cow? Where do I get those? I don't want anyone to know—"

"Yeah, yeah, no one can know you're here. Big deal." Emily waved her hand at him. "I had a cow that lost her calf this spring. You could have milked her by hand."

"What?" Jake sat up a little straighter in the tub, forgetting his weakness and pain in this new horror.

"I'll show you, although I'm not too good at it myself. I could wean one of my calves early and bottle-feed it. The cows don't have enough milk for both." She considered it for a moment, then shook her head emphatically. "No, that won't work. My cows are just too wild."

"I've seen your cows come crowding into the yard at feeding time. They don't seem wild to me."

"Well, you haven't tried to grab one by the—"

"I'm not much of a milk drinker really," Jake interjected.

"You've got to have a cow to live off the land. It's a renewable source of food that stays fresh as long—" Emily snickered. "As long as it stays inside the cow."

"What's so funny?"

"I'm imagining you milking a cow, that's all. It's not funny because I'll probably get my head kicked off trying to train the cow to put up with it. Then you'll get to drink all the milk."

"They kick?"

Emily groaned and let her forehead drop onto her knees. She rested for a minute, then seemed to rally.

Jake silently scolded himself for asking so many questions. And determined that from this moment on he'd just say things like, "Yes, Emily," and, "Whatever you say, Emily."

"You'll need chickens, and for them you just have to have electricity."

"No, absolutely not. Out of the question. I'm not going to get electricity hooked up, I told you—"

"Okay, okay, let me think." She looked up at him fiercely.

He remembered his vow of obedience. Okay, starting now.

"I know Laura Ingalls Wilder's pa didn't have electricity. Let me think." She glared at him. "I don't know how to live off the land myself, you know. The natural way would be to have a mother hen hatch some chicks, and you can do that. But what this boils down to is which comes first, the chicken or the egg. I think it has to be the chicken. I'll buy baby chicks and you can let them grow up and you can raise your own generation of them from those chickens. But the first generation has no mother, so you have to have a heat lamp."

"Can't I just buy a pregnant chicken?"

Emily started to laugh so hard she let go of her knees and flopped over backward onto the floor. She rested her hands over her stomach and laughed, and as much as Jake wanted to toss the soggy towel on her face, he was beginning to get the swing of this mature-adult-in-control-of-himself thing.

"Would you mind telling me what's so funny?" He thought his voice was the very model of respect, however totally she was failing on her side.

"Pregnant chickens?" She barely uttered the words before she was lost again.

It was hard to tell, his being so hot from a sunburn, but he thought he might be blushing. "Look, I know chickens hatch from eggs, okay? I meant a chicken ready to lay eggs that would hatch." He sounded a bit testy, but he still had control.

"It just sounded so funny." Emily still couldn't coordinate herself well enough to sit up.

Jake was severely tempted to get out of the tub and grab her and— He'd counted to ten for the fifth time when she suddenly quit laughing.

"What did you do to the ceiling?" From her position flat on her back she had noticed his pride and joy.

He grabbed desperately at the change of subject. "It's pressed tin. I'm going to put it in the kitchen, too. I'm trying to blend the true Victorian style with modern amenities all through the house."

Emily sat up, wiping tears from her eyes, and looked around some more. She ran her hand over the tiled floor. "This is real tile. You didn't use linoleum."

"I chose the pattern and laid it."

"It's beautiful. You designed it yourself? It's so intricate it must have taken days." Her eyes shone with pleasure.

He thought he saw the first inkling of respect he'd ever gotten from her and it helped dispel the immature desire to get her to quit laughing at him by kissing her. "It's how a Victorian home should look. The ceiling was something I ordered from a specialty catalogue at the Home Depot in Rapid City. I've been to town for supplies a couple of times."

"What do you do, sneak out before sunrise so no one sees you?"

"Yes, with the trailer. I can load a lot of stuff in it. I'm in town before the doors open at seven. Then I get home as fast as I can."

"Someone's going to notice you. This can't last."

Jake shrugged. "I've found a route that's out of the way, and it doesn't go past any houses until I get to a bigger highway. I think I am going to make my own ceiling for the kitchen. I've looked at this one and I think I know how to do it. I made the heavy cornices." He pointed to the ceiling again.

"You mean the molding along the ceiling and the wall? You carved all that wood?" Emily sat with her legs crossed at the ankles, looking at all the details.

He loved it that she was impressed. "It's not carved, though that's the effect I wanted. I added quarter round and a small molding to the largest molding I could find, and nailed it together. The leaf pattern is plaster stenciled to match the leaves in the tin ceiling. I painted the whole thing white. That's how a lot of Victorian houses were, so I didn't cheat on the ceiling, but I did on the fixtures."

Emily ran her hand across the odd wrought iron legs that held up the cream and white marble sink. "It looks ancient. It wasn't in here before."

"No, and it's not an antique. It's got all the strength of porcelain, it looks and feels like marble, and it's really plastic. Since I got it, I found some catalogues I might use to buy antique pieces, but I wanted the bathroom to be functional. I did save the commode though. I tore out all the insides and put in new, but I couldn't part with that cast iron lion."

"I always loved that lion. I never missed a chance to come in here and talk to him." Emily ran her hand over the ridiculous white lion sitting proudly, creating the base for a toilet. "It was just another way this house made me feel like a princess when I played over here." Her eyes drifted back up to the ceiling.

"The Barretts were so nice to me. When I think of how they let me have the run of this place. . ." Emily dropped her eyes from the ceiling and touched again the mosaic of earth-toned floor tiles. "I know what this reminds me of. My grandma made a quilt that looks just like this."

He saw the sentiment in her gaze, and he was glad she had been in time to save her tree. He suspected she'd like the source of his floor motif, too. When he picked it, he had just done it to suit his own taste, but now it seemed like he'd done it to pay his respects to one of Emily's ancestors. "I saw the quilt. That's where I got the idea."

Emily looked up, confused. "When did you see it?"

"The day you took out my stickers. It's thrown over your couch in the living room. It looked just like something I'd been playing around with in my head, the squares and triangles combined in these shades." He continued to bathe himself, feeling almost normal. He looked at the red skin of his arms and knew he'd pay for this act of idiocy for days.

She looked up to catch him studying his burn. "How are we ever going to keep you alive?"

"You're going to help me. Starting with getting me a pregnant chicken." He scowled at her, daring her to laugh.

She didn't let his scowl slow down her giggling at all. "So, you know where chickens come from? That's good. You'll still need chicks and a heat lamp. The Barretts' old brooder house will take some repairs to keep the rats and weasels out."

"Rats and weasels?" The horror at having to fight off rats must have been noticeable because he saw she wasn't impressed. In fact, if he wasn't mistaken, she was trying valiantly not to start laughing again. "What kind of place is this?"

"And snakes. Don't forget snakes. Life is hard on something as defenseless as baby chicks. The truth is you probably need a dog and a couple of cats. They keep the pests away as well as anything. Of course they like to eat chicks, too, but you can usually fence them out."

"Dogs and cats and cows and chickens." And suddenly through all the annoying details, Jake's dream came back to him. He really wanted all of this. He wanted huge orange pumpkins, a friendly dog, and a cat that would curl itself around his leg while he read by the fireplace at night.

The humor that had been lurking under the surface warmed in Emily's eyes and, for just a minute, he thought she almost shared his dream.

Then she went and spoiled everything by talking. "You'll have to have electricity."

"No. I told you—"

"The chicks have to have a heat lamp. It's a substitute for their mother sitting on top of them. They won't survive even on warm days without it." She was trying so hard to be reasonable.

He had no intention of letting her get away with being reasonable. "No power. No way. That's final."

"The chicks will die."

"We'll skip the chickens. We'll just do the rest."

"But chickens are the only quick source of protein I can think of. The eggs and the meat. You can't butcher a cow or pig without a freezer to store the meat. But you can kill a chicken and eat it all in one day, so the meat never spoils."

"Kill it? I thought I was going to eat eggs."

"The girls lay eggs and the boys you eat."

Jake's fist hit the water. "Who invented that sick system?"

"What other use are the boys? That is their purpose in life. It's been years, but I think I remember how to chop off their heads with an ax."

Jake surged to his feet. He was self-aware enough to know a fight-or-flight reflex had kicked in. "I'm not going to chop something's head off with an ax." Water swished over the sides of the tub when he stood. "What is *wrong* with you?"

Emily rose, dodging most of the water. "I thought you wanted to live off the land? Do you really think the chickens in the store are from noble chickens who, after a full life and a death from natural causes, donated their bodies to grocery stores?" She stepped way too close to him and about did him in when she poked him in the chest. "Just because you're going to be intimately involved in their deaths doesn't make them any more dead than the ones hermetically sealed on Styrofoam trays. It's where meat comes from, hotshot."

Hotshot really set him off, and for one tense moment he forgot his pledge to treat Emily better. His hands clenched as he stopped himself from grabbing that irritating finger.

Something blazed between them. Emily dropped her hand without his making her. She wavered a minute and he wasn't sure if she was going to step away or lean into him.

For once he wanted to go first. He sat back down in the icy water. It was the best place for him.

When he finally glanced up, she looked relieved and surprised and maybe just one tiny speck disappointed. He went back to cooling himself off, deeply proud of his self-control.

Letting her teach him just might work. But he didn't think he could kill a chicken. He'd wait and give her the bad news later.

She cleared her throat. "About electricity. . ."

"No." He loved that word. He was going to be saying it to himself pretty regularly in the coming days. He might as well bury her with it, too. For an instant he remembered his "Yes, Emily. Whatever you say, Emily," pledge but dismissed it. A man had to have some fun. He'd start being obedient as soon as they settled the electricity question.

"How about an extension cord? I could buy a few hundred yards of heavy duty extension cords and run them from my place."

"No."

"A generator. I have one of those, gas powered. We'd just run it overnight for a week or two, for the chicks. Or I could raise the chicks until they're past the age of needing heat and send them over to you."

"No, I'll raise them here. I'll find a heat source."

"Chicks don't respond well to a wood fire," she informed him sarcastically. "All you'll get for your trouble is a barbecue. Let me start them. I'll let you come over and do everything, I promise. In fact, I insist."

He really wanted to say no again, but he was starting to bore himself. "We'll figure something out. I'll give you the money and you buy the cow and chicks and—"

"We'll worry about the money later. That's enough at first. No more gardening today. Why don't you rest for the afternoon and come for supper tonight?"

"Can we have apple pie again?"

"I've got a busy afternoon." She smiled and the words had no bite.

"But you said they were easy, remember?" And he couldn't believe how pathetic he sounded. He couldn't ever remember caring much about food before.

"Not a chance, bud. I have a roast in the Crock-Pot. It's been slow-cooking since noon. It's not no-dessert tonight, but you'll like what I make well enough, I suppose."

"I'm sure of it." Jake lifted the towel to his face and breathed cool air through the soaking cloth. It was probably time to get out of the tub. His skin didn't hurt so badly, and he had a permanent case of goose bumps.

He lowered the towel. "You've saved me again. This time, I promise, is the last. From now on I'll consult with you before I start anything."

"It's not all your fault you didn't consult me. I haven't made it easy."

Those eyes were so deep with all of her feminine power and softness that he wanted to get lost in them. Instead, he slapped himself a little bit too hard with the dripping towel. He wasn't going to get lost. Not anymore. Not now that maybe he was finally finding himself. He was a changed man. "You've done the right thing all along. Now I'm going to help you instead of working against you. I'm going to listen and learn."

She leaned over to rest one callused hand on his forehead, testing his skin temperature. He wondered if she was checking for a fever because his being so decent to her came off as delirium.

And after just a bit more fussing and advice, she went. All the while she was smiling so sweetly he knew he could get another pie without any trouble at all.

fifteen

The morning after Jake's brush with heatstroke, an insistent rapping on the door woke him at 8:00 a.m.

Every muscle in his body ached as he thrust himself out of bed and into his jeans and blue chambray shirt.

Stumbling to his front door barefoot, he reminded himself he was going to be friendly.

He had made a steadfast civility oath and he was going to keep it or die trying. Right now, with her irritating habit of waking him up, seemed like a good time to start. He breathed in a long patient breath and opened the door. "Good morning." There was no need to fake sincerity, he was too sincerely delighted. "You brought me a cow?"

Emily held a lead rope connected to a small black and white cow and carried a large box under her arm that emitted ominous squeaking sounds. "A cow and some baby chicks."

"Are you okay this morning?" Stephie stood behind her with a little red wagon overflowing with two big paper bags and a small cooler.

"I'm sorry if we woke you. You had a hard day yesterday." Emily didn't seem to have any real remorse.

But Jake didn't complain as they fussed pleasantly over his sunburn and his general health until he was thoroughly ashamed of his irritation. He silently vowed they'd never catch him sleeping again. Jake started down the veranda steps.

Emily tied the cow to the corner railing. "Go get your boots on, cowboy, while the womenfolk make breakfast."

Jake tipped an imaginary Stetson, noting Emily's real one. He needed a cowboy hat, too, now that he had a cow. "Much obliged, ma'am." He hurried back inside, eager to start this day.

Using only Emily's little camping stove and ingredients they brought along, they made him a huge breakfast of bacon and eggs and pancakes in the time it took him to brush his teeth and pull on his boots. Emily insisted he sit long enough to drink a second cup of coffee out of her thermos before they took him outside to display their purchases.

The cow chewed her cud placidly as Emily stroked her back. "This is the gentlest cow I could find. I know the boy who raised her. She was his 4-H project and he took her to the fair last year, so she's been handled a lot. Never milked by hand though."

Fear chilled Jake's overcooked skin. How gentle was gentle? "Do we milk her right now?"

Stephie grinned as she tipped the sacks out of her wagon. "She's gonna have a baby. You can't milk her till it's born."

"A baby. . .really? Don't cows have their babies in the spring? You said yours did." Jake, reprieved from climbing under the cow, looked forward to the calf.

Emily nodded as she set the noisy box on the grass, well away from the heifer's hooves. "Beef cattle do, but not Holsteins. A dairy farmer calves year round. This will be her first calf. Holsteins give enough milk for a baby with plenty to share with you. She's been handled a lot, so we ought to be able to milk her." Emily managed to look doubtful and determined at the same time.

Jake loved the way Emily said "we."

Stephie set off back into the trees with the wagon. Jake wanted to ask her what she needed to get and maybe help her. The feed had been a pretty heavy load, but the conspiratorial look that passed between Stephie and Emily kept him still. Stephie obviously wanted to surprise him, so he'd let her.

"See that weird little roof over there?" Emily pointed to something he'd dismissed as a collapsed shed. Weeds were grown up around it. "It's a brooder house. We need to drag it out of the tall grass and patch it."

It was about two feet tall, including a foot of gradually sloping roof. She helped him pull it across the ground to a grassy spot. With a tact that delighted him, she plunked down a sack full of small boards, a hammer, and nails, then gave him the respect of offering no direction. Instead she carried the feed sacks to the barn.

She stayed a long time in the barn, and when she returned, she opened the top of the squeaking box.

Suddenly the air was full of the tiny high-pitched cheeps. He laid his tools aside and looked in at dozens of baby chicks. They looked like bright yellow cotton balls with legs. Legs and vocal cords. He reached into the box and jumped back when all of them tried to peck him at once.

Emily laughed and picked one up.

To restore his manly pride, he boldly took a chick of his own and soon realized that the pecking and scratching tickled more than it hurt. Up close he could see the yellow fuzz was thinning in spots and little white feathers were growing in place of the fluff.

Emily took out a little flat tray, opened a section of the brooder house roof that was hinged, set the tray in, and then knelt by the brooder house to pour a jar full of water into the tray.

"They're white leghorns. They'll be good egg layers. Here, watch. We need to give each of them a drink before we let them go." She picked up a chick and dipped its beak in the water, then tipped the chick upward as if the water could only get down its throat using gravity.

"Why?"

Emily straightened away from the water, still holding the chick. "I don't know. I just remember my mom and grandma doing it." She grinned, then set the chick in the brooder house, caught another one, and dipped its beak.

Before she set the second chick down, the first had escaped through a hole. "Now you know where to patch." She smiled again.

He had to scramble to get the building patched. Some escape routes were so tiny he'd have never considered them.

When the chicks were all settled and drinking and safely trapped inside, Emily led the cow to a fenced-in yard around another old building that was almost swallowed up by the trees. He'd been so busy with the house, he hadn't spared any thought to the half dozen little shacks scattered around his place. He'd explored the hulking old barn a bit, but Emily seemed delighted with the existence of every building.

Stephie came back down the forest path.

Jake was startled to see a wriggling brown creature in her wagon that he couldn't identify. It looked like a fifty-pound worm.

When she got closer, he couldn't look at the wagon because he was so overwhelmed by the angelic smile on Stephie's face. She pulled the wagon with tender care, and he could tell she was dying to show him her cargo, so her caution was all the more impressive. She stopped next to him. "Are the chicks safe? Can they get out anymore?" She asked the question with terrible seriousness.

He forced down his curiosity and checked the little building again. "I have it sealed up now."

Stephie closed the door that swung up out of the brooder house roof, then she quickly opened what Jake now recognized as a gunny sack, and produced two half-grown kittens. "Aren't they cute?" She hugged each of them close, then handed them to Jake.

He took only one because he could tell she couldn't bear to give up both. He heard the loud purring coming from the yellow-and-white-striped kitten in Stephie's arms and was honored that his little gray one started in with the same contented rumbling against his chest.

Emily came up behind Stephie and watched the whole proceeding with a big smile. "Always feed them in the barn. Then they'll live out there. Feed them one time, just one single time," she warned ominously, "outside your back door, and you've got house cats. And then you have to get more cats for the outside and they'll all want to be house cats, too."

"Where can we put them, Em?" Stephie's question told Jake there was more to come.

"There's going to be fireworks no matter what we do, so I guess just put them down on the ground. We might as well get it over with." Emily gave the brooder house a quick once-over as Stephie set her kitten on the rough grass like it was a china figurine and turned to untie another sack on the wagon. "You'd better put yours down, too, Jake. You might get scratched."

He obeyed her because he had promised himself he would let her be boss. He was glad he'd turned it loose when Stephie withdrew her hands from the bag holding a squirming puppy.

He greeted freedom with sharp little yips that pierced the air and sent the kittens flying across the lawn in a frenzy to get away from the noisy little pup. Eventually the gray one ended up in the branches of Emily's American elm tree and the tiger kitten disappeared into the shed with his cow. His cow. His chickens. His cats. His puppy. Jake couldn't stop smiling.

Stephie struggled with the hyperactive little creature, and Jake laughed out loud at the antics as the brown-and-white fur ball alternately licked Stephie's giggling mouth and tried desperately to get away.

"Puppies are trouble, Jake. I almost regret getting you one. But they're so cute you forgive them, and he'll keep the varmints away. Don't leave anything outside you don't want chewed up and buried. Especially boots." Emily, despite her hard words, couldn't keep the smile off her face.

Stephie sat down on the grass and let the puppy jump all over her.

Jake was surprised at his pleasure over the puppy. He'd never had a dog. Until this moment he'd never wanted one. "He's great. I want to hear all about everything. I can't believe you got so much done so quickly."

"Well, puppies and kittens come easily, although I think I got you good ones. The kittens come from a great mouser on the farm where I got the cow. The puppy was advertised in the Hot Springs paper. He's the result of an unfortunate encounter between a purebred bloodhound and an Airedale. So he'll either be the world's calmest rodent-hating dog, which would be fantastic, or he'll be a bundle of nerves who bays at the moon all night and sleeps all day—that could get old. One thing's for sure, he's going to be big, and even if it's just the noise he'll make, he ought to keep raccoons and possums away from the chicks."

"I thought it was rats and weasels," Jake interjected.

Emily smiled and shrugged. "Them, too. The trouble is the puppy may want to eat the chicks himself at first, and if we ever let him get one, it'll be really hard to break him of the habit. So it's important to keep the chicks locked up in the brooder house. The kittens will be happy to snack on them, too. Six weeks from now the chicks will be full grown, but the pup and kittens will still be babies, and the chickens will be able to push them around. Until then we have to be on guard.

"The chicks were in a farm supply store in Hot Springs. Stephie always wants to play with them when we're there, so today was a thrill."

"You've done all this before I ever got out of bed." Jake had thought he was a slacker when they caught him sleeping. Now he knew it.

"You had a tough day yesterday. You needed to rest." Emily went on talking with no sign of the censure he knew he deserved. "The family that raised your heifer lives close to Hot Springs. That's why I went there. I took a field road that doesn't pass any homes to get back to my place, so none of the neighbors saw me drive by with the heifer in my truck. Chances are the word won't get around that I bought her. You should still be a secret."

Jake wondered how difficult it had been for her to pick a route home so she wouldn't be seen. He was asking too much of her. And what about money? "This must have cost a fortune."

"Don't worry. I'm planning to let you repay me. Although if you have more eggs than you need in a few months, we'll help you eat them, so I don't mind splitting the cost of the chickens. The cow cost the most. That kid really valued his cow." Emily raised her eyebrows in mock fear. "She can never give enough milk to pay for herself."

"That's okay. I'm not going to try to squeeze a bargain out of a little boy." Jake noticed that Emily was concerned over spending too much of his money without his approval. That was a totally unique experience for him with a woman.

"We have cat food and dog food and I'll bring the mash over for the chicks in a minute." Emily ticked purchases off on her fingers.

Stephie jumped up from her frolicking and thrust the puppy into Jake's hands. "I'll get the next load."

He had been dying to pet the little fellow, but he hadn't wanted to ask Stephie to part with him. Now he was thrilled as his hands sank into the soft fur while the puppy panted and yipped, and in the background, fifty tiny peeps amounted to a roar.

Stephie walked off pulling the rattling little wagon.

Over the din was Emily's steady instruction. He looked at her and saw intelligence and grace as she shared with him the life she loved.

He had to lift the puppy in front of his face. His behavior was going to be exemplary, but Emily the helpful teacher was even more compelling than Emily the crabby neighbor. And he'd been dangerously attracted to the crabby version, so he was in trouble.

He held the pup under its rotund tummy and hooked his thumbs around its front legs. Then he looked eye to eye with his new companion, its tongue hanging out. Jake even let the little wiggler lick his cheek just to get his mind on something besides how lovely Emily looked in her work boots and braid.

And how, with no makeup or expensive clothing, she enhanced the natural beauty he found all around him and became the center of it.

Her fingers brushed against his hands and he wondered if she could possibly be experiencing all that he was. Her hands seemed to slip over his, and as she touched him he gave serious thought to forgetting all his noble promises, especially if she wasn't interested in behaving.

"Quit hogging the puppy." She slid her hands past his and around the dog.

Jake was as jealous as he'd ever been in his life. But he released his hold on the squirming little hound.

"The chicks will eat the grass from under the brooder house. You'll need to move it every day so they're always on clean ground. Stephie's bringing a waterer. The store even sold them to me for a bargain because people usually want the younger chicks. Since they're a little older and the forecast sounds warm, they'll probably be okay without a heat lamp."

Jake watched Emily let the puppy win his struggle to be free. It scampered away and immediately began happily terrorizing the chicks by jumping against the side of the brooder house, barking in pure frenzy.

Emily grabbed him by the scruff of the neck and deflected his attention by kneeling beside him and rolling him over to tickle his tummy. "I'm sorry about all this. I don't know how you'll manage. I shouldn't have brought everything at once."

Jake wanted to roll her over and tickle her tummy. He wanted to laugh and touch the softness of the chicks and wrestle with his pup. He wanted to find out what was involved in delivering a baby calf. "I don't know how I'm going to do it either, but I can't wait to try. I'm really living off the land now."

Jake was used to menacing cracks sagging over his head and buckling under his feet as he assessed damage from some natural disaster or, in a few terrible cases, bombs. He was used to people—pleading people, suffering people, dying people. He was used to his heart pounding with the pressure and peril and despair.

The country life was solitary and quiet. Progress was as slow as watching a seed come up or an animal grow. He noticed the absence of the pounding heart and rubbed his hand over his chest as he thought about the price his father had paid for making work the center of his life. He hoped he'd finally made a break from the trail his father had blazed.

"Yes, I think maybe you're a pioneer now, hotshot."

Their eyes met and, for Jake, it was a perfect moment. The young life all around him. The sweetness of Stephie's little voice as she made her way back to them, singing. And the beautiful, teasing woman who couldn't keep from caressing a puppy even as she listed off the dire trouble the little sprout would cause.

His eyes rose to the branches of the American elm tree that swayed over his head, and he thanked God that Emily had stopped him before he could chop it down.

He thanked God.

In that perfect moment, a thousand random twists and turns that had led him to this place all locked together. What had once seemed like a life lived randomly was in fact just pieces of a jigsaw puzzle that now came together. He hadn't just been wandering aimlessly all this time. He'd been traveling to here and now. The sum of his experience had prepared him to appreciate where he was with a full heart. A full, healthy heart.

"You know something?" With all the easy camaraderie that had typified this morning, he could tell when she looked up at him that she knew it was important.

"What?"

"God led me here. God put me right here."

"And that surprises you?"

Jake almost laughed. He expected her to be awed. Instead, she accepted it easily. Of course God put him here. It was just another thing to love about this life—the "of course" about God.

"I hadn't thought of it in years, but I remember now, after my mom left and I realized how alone I was, I used to pray. I'd lie in bed at night and know my father wouldn't be home before I went to sleep. And he'd be gone when I woke up. I'd pray for someone to come in and care about me."

Emily started to stand from where she sat cross-legged on the grass, but he raised a hand to stop her. He wanted to finish and he knew if he let her, she'd hold him, and he was too vulnerable to keep his resolutions if she was in his arms.

She stopped when he signaled, but she was there. And knowing it made all the difference. It gave him the courage to remember.

"I must have prayed that same prayer for a year before I finally gave up. It was how I put myself to sleep at night. I'd talk to God about my mom. Our housekeeper told me she had a new husband. I'd ask God to make her come for me. Or I'd pray for my father to come in, just once, and tuck me in bed. We had live-in help that took care of me. The one that was there when Mom left was really kind. She'd come in and read me stories and help me say my prayers. But Dad changed hired help constantly, and before I knew it she was gone, and the new housekeeper didn't like bothering with me. I kept saying my prayers though. Not just for my parents but even for the housekeeper to come. Anything to break up that aloneness."

"Jake, I'm so sorry." Her compassion washed away the pain of his reflection.

Jake looked at her and smiled. "Don't be. I'm not feeling sorry for myself. I just realized I wasn't alone all those long, dark nights. God was with me. He was always there. I knew it then." He knelt next to her in the grass, just as Stephie came into the clearing. He reached for the puppy to keep himself from reaching for Emily. "Hope hurt too much after a while. So I quit asking, quit praying. But by doing that, I see now I shut out the only One who was there."

Emily smiled up at him, but he saw a sheen of tears in her

eyes. Whatever she saw in his expression, helped to keep her tears from spilling.

"I've found Him again, Emily. I want to say He's here, here on this ranch. But the truth is He's been with me everywhere. I'm the one who quit talking. I'm the one who made my loneliness come true. But I'm never going to be alone again. This time I'm keeping Him close."

"When you're done being a secret, you can come to our church. It's a country church with lovely people in it. I think you'd like them. They'd welcome you. You'd make friends, Christian friends who'd be interested in you for yourself, not your money. You never have to be alone again."

Their eyes met.

Jake knew then, with God in his heart and Emily in his arms and little Stephie at his side, he had already left his lonely life behind. His eyes locked with hers and too much passed between them to ignore.

Stephie arrived with her latest load. Jake rose, the puppy in one hand, and reached down with the other to assist his lovely neighbor to her feet. "Get up and teach me what to do with all these animals. Then I'll come over and help you with your chores. You must be hours behind."

Emily hesitated, but she looked from his outstretched hand to his smiling eyes and, with the generosity he'd come to expect from her, she reached out to him. He pulled her to her feet, and just for a second she was too close.

"Can I hold the puppy?" Stephie begged.

Jake dropped Emily's hand. He turned to Stephie and, needing to find an acceptable way to express his joy, he gave her the little dog, then swished Stephie off her feet and swung her and the puppy around in the air until they were helpless with laughter.

sixteen

A new neighbor had moved in next door.

There was no other way to describe it. Whoever lived there wasn't Jake. No one could change like he had.

Or maybe it was fairer to say this was Jake, and whoever had lived there before was gone. She had to admit she'd seen flashes of this relaxed, kind gentleman over the weeks, especially around Stephie. But now there seemed to be nothing left of the old. Like a butterfly emerging from its cocoon, Jake had transformed into something wonderful.

He was at her house constantly. He ate all his meals there, including breakfast. He prayed fervently before he ate each meal, taking over the prayers as if he were head of the household.

He did so many of her chores she felt guilty, and he had more patience with Stephie than Emily did. Stephie and she were at his house every day, fussing over the chicks and trying in vain to train the puppy.

The chicks grew with startling speed. By the end of June, they'd changed from precious, fragile babies into clucking scavengers. Emily was relieved that they got by without the heat because she knew Jake would feel terrible if they died.

Emily decided to force Jake to accept one tiny modern convenience. She showed up at his house one morning with a portable bottle of propane. The dog barked like crazy when she came over, but Jake didn't wake up. What was the point of having a guard dog if you slept through his alarm?

She sneaked into his basement through the sloped cellar door, then hooked the little bottle of gas into the hot water heater in the belly of Jake's castle. She lit the heater without his seeing her.

Later in the morning, she turned on the tap. "Welcome to the twenty-first century, Jake."

Jake looked up from the kitchen table where he and Stephie were taking a milk and cookie break. "What do you mean?"

The faucet began to steam.

"Hot water."

Jake rose slowly from the table.

Emily waited for the explosion. To head it off, she said, "A hot shower will feel great."

He caved with only a token fight and Emily knew he was a goner. He'd taken the first step down the slippery slope of convenience.

Later, as Emily plotted what to force on him next—a gas stove maybe—she realized she pictured herself cooking at his stove. With a sinking heart, she admitted to herself she cared about him. It wasn't friendship anymore.

And he was leaving.

seventeen

He was staying forever!

Jake grinned as he tossed a bale of hay high in the air, clearing the wooden fence by several feet. The cows shoved their way close to the feeder set on the other side of the fence as he grabbed the next bale. They chomped and snorted as they shoved their way to the feed. He could throw bales so much faster than Emily she didn't even help anymore.

He loved it. In this one tiny area of his life he was better at ranching than Emily. Enjoying the pressure on his muscles as he heaved another bale, he knew it was silly to gloat, but he wanted to be in Emily's league. He wanted to know everything there was to know. Not just memorize the chores to be done but understand all the whys.

He wanted to sing out loud and shout praises to God. His reawakened faith was the best part of this lifestyle change. Yes, even better than Emily and Stephie, because he could care about them more with God in charge of his life. And the more he learned about Emily, the more he cared.

He tried to conjure up indignation when she sneaked over and started up his hot water heater. How could she believe he hadn't heard her with Lucky's yipping? He'd almost called a halt to the gambit when she crept into his basement. She was breaking and entering, trespassing, plumbing without a license. Some of those were felonies. But before he generated the gumption to get out of bed and get dressed and go scold her, he thought of how great a hot shower would feel, and he decided they weren't really *important* felonies. He'd bent his arms behind his head and nestled deeper into his pillow to listen contentedly to her clanking around in his basement.

The last bale delivered to the greedy cattle, he tugged his leather work gloves off his hands and watched the big, placid animals crowd around the feed bunk. He heard the soft munching of their teeth against the bristling hay. He looked across the feedlot and watched Emily's three-month-old calves frolic on the hillside. Beyond the rolling pastures of Emily's land, the majestic peaks of the Black Hills stretched for miles. All around this clearing, tree branches rustled in the late afternoon July breeze.

A beautiful place, a beautiful life. He wondered what amazing, fresh-vegetable-rich feast Emily was making for supper. The peas and radishes and leaf lettuce were gone now, but there were new potatoes and green beans, and the tomatoes hung heavy on the vine, a few showing the first tantalizing blush as they promised to turn from green to red.

He tucked his gloves behind his belt buckle the way Emily did it, and enjoyed the sights, the sounds, the smells. The warmth of the afternoon sun on his denim-covered back felt great. His skin had finished peeling and he used caution now. He was learning.

He ran one hand over his chest and let the strong beat of his heart reassure him that this was the life for him, not the burning, dying, high-stakes existence he had abandoned.

Scampering footsteps warned him of the approach of Stephie and Lucky. "Did Cowlick have her baby?" Stephie skidded to a halt in front of him. She'd been asking him that same question a half-dozen times a day. Jake couldn't help but be amused by her fascination, considering the dozens of calves right in front of her.

"Not last time I looked. I was heading home now. Want to go with me to check?"

"Sure. I'll tell Emily." Stephie ran off as fast as she'd come, and Jake started for home, knowing Emily would say yes. Lucky nipped at Stephie's heels, and Jake admitted who the dog belonged to. Jake didn't mind. He was over here as often as the dog.

By the time Jake crested the hill toward his house, Stephie caught up and slid her hand into his with her usual breezy friendliness.

Preoccupied with his enjoyment of the day, he didn't notice anything different as he stepped in the barn. By the time his eyes adjusted to the slightly darker interior of the old building, Stephie had run back outside to check the pen.

She dashed inside, grabbed his hand, and hauled him into the sunlight. "She's gone. Cowlick's gone!"

Rustlers!

A frantic look around the little yard where his heifer lazed her life away, awaiting the blessed event, revealed no cow. Someone had come onto his place in broad daylight, because he'd checked Cowlick just a couple of hours ago. Rustlers had driven away his entire herd. No one would get away with this bold assault on his property. He'd hunt for tracks. He'd form a posse. Hanging was too good for—

"She's having her baby."

Jake looked up from hunting for tracks. "How do you know that?"

Stephie pointed to the ten-foot gap in his fence. "Look, she's knocked that big wooden gate down over there. I know 'cuz cows run off to be by themselves when they're gonna have babies. They do it at our place all the time."

He'd have noticed in a minute. He couldn't read all the signs at once.

"Come on. Let's get Emily and go look for her."

It irritated him to go running to Emily for help. Maybe because he had appeared a teensy bit stupid to not spot the missing gate. "Why do we need to get Emily? She says the cow doesn't need any help. She's told me that a hundred times." A couple hundred, because he'd been worrying and he'd asked and asked and asked.

"Well, we should find Cowlick and bring her back, or at least make sure she hasn't wandered too far. I guess we could go alone." Stephie looked at him with such doubt in her eyes that Jake waged a war with his wounded manhood.

Stephie adored him. She thought he could do no wrong. If she thought they needed Emily, they probably did. And he had taken a solemn oath to never scare Stephie or almost get himself killed again. Now might be his first chance to prove he possessed a learning curve. "Okay, let's go get Emily."

Five minutes later, Emily crawled out from under her hay baler and deserted whatever adjustments she was making. "There's no fence for miles to the north so she could be anywhere, but my guess is she didn't go far."

Cowlick was over the crest of the first hill south of his house, standing so close to the fence she could touch noses with Emily's cows if they wandered to that side of the pasture. For now, Cowlick was completely apart. Jake wondered if cows got lonely.

"Yep, she's calving for sure." Emily absently dusted grime from her hands without taking her eyes off the mother-to-be.

"She's just standing there. How do you know she's in labor?"

Emily laughed at him for no reason he could understand. "Because she's just standing there, that's how I know."

Her amusement pinched more than it should. "That doesn't tell me anything. You're supposed to be teaching me." He should be used to being the dumb one.

She quit laughing. "Sorry, you're right. I don't mean to go laughing at your question. What she's doing isn't normal. So, I'm sure she's calving. What made me laugh is *labor*. I'm not used to thinking of cattle that way. They're a long way from humans when it comes to babies. The mama stands there and the baby is born. No birthing classes, no doctor in a white coat. Right now I'd like to shoo her on back to your barn. Being out here is just an old instinct. It doesn't do her any good. I'd rather have her close up to the place."

Jake shook his head in disbelief at Emily's insensitivity. "We can't make her walk all that way. It's cruel."

"What's cruel is letting her have the baby out here and then making you carry the slippery little thing back to the barn on those big broad shoulders of yours, hotshot. I say let her tote the little tyke in before it's born. Besides, if she has any difficulties, my doctoring stuff is back there. Let's go."

"Doctoring stuff? Wait. . .what difficulties? I thought you said—" He was talking to himself.

Stephie headed up the hill, and Emily followed. Jake went along but he thought the whole idea of making a lady in the throes of calf-birth take a long walk was barbaric. They headed Cowlick toward the barn. She strolled along like she didn't have a care in the world. By the time they had her locked up, Jake had decided they were wrong about the baby being delivered any time soon.

"Let's grab an early supper, then come back and check her. I'm guessing you want to see the whole thing, right Jake?" Emily hefted the ten-foot panel back into place without asking for help. She found some baling wire and was half done securing it before Jake could lend a hand.

"Weeellll…" Jake shrugged his shoulders sheepishly, suddenly feeling like a voyeur. "Yeah."

"Okay, it'll be a while, so let's eat, feed the chickens, and tie Lucky up. He might make the new mama nervous if he comes in at the wrong time." With a final tug at the fence, Emily glanced at him for agreement, and they headed back to the Johannson ranch.

eighteen

Jake barely tasted the new potatoes, steaming and tender, boiled with their skins on, that he and Stephie had dug. He nearly swallowed the crunchy, perfectly undercooked green beans whole even though he'd helped snap them. He had seconds of everything and a third grilled hamburger, just so it wouldn't go to waste.

He did slow down to savor the cherry cobbler Emily had made with the last of the cherries from her own tree. He'd helped freeze a couple of dozen quarts of cherries and Emily had taught him how to make jelly, then given him half of the jars. She put food like this on the table for every meal. Whatever was ripe in the garden.

He was trying to cut back on his lavish compliments because she would look at him like he was some lab specimen when he marveled at her cooking. But on the rare occasion he held the gushing flattery, he could tell she missed it.

Today, since Cowlick was probably in desperate need of him, he kept it to a minimum.

❧

Hay hung from the corners of Cowlick's mouth when they reentered. She gave them a bored look and kept chewing.

Jake and Stephie began petting the cow's head while Emily turned her attention immediately to the business end of birth.

"Uh oh. Those aren't front feet."

"Do you have to pull it, Emily?" Stephie was an old pro.

It was Jake Emily was worried about. She didn't have time to hold his hand.

"Is there something wrong?" Jake came around to Emily's side, then staggered backward, gasping.

120

Two legs protruding from the back end of a cow could be a shock for a greenhorn. "Stephie, toss a scoop of corn in Cowlick's feeder. Let's get her in the head gate." She slapped the heifer on her back, urging her forward.

"Don't hit her!" Jake grabbed her wrist.

Emily smiled. "Cows have a tough hide. I'm not hurting her."

Jake held tight. "Can't we get her to move without that?"

Emily's temper flared. "This calf is coming backward, and the longer it stays inside of her, the greater the chance of losing it. Let go." She held his gaze until he reluctantly dropped her arm.

Out of respect for Jake, she clapped the cow gently on her back, then a little harder. Cowlick didn't budge. Stephie poured corn into the feeder, and the heifer stuck her head through the open head gate. Emily leaned forward to slide the stanchion shut around Cowlick's neck. The cow ignored them and ate her grain.

Emily dragged a heavy apparatus across the barn, along with a toolbox she had converted to a veterinary kit.

Jake looked anxiously at the six-foot-long, Y-shaped metal brace with its dangling chain. "Where did that stuff come from?"

"I moved it over here a while ago." She upended a plastic bucket, then set it down, disconnected the chain from the brace, and dropped the chain in the bucket.

"You mean you knew there was going to be a problem?"

Rummaging in the vet kit she'd also moved over here earlier, she produced a pint bottle of iodine and poured most of the dark yellow liquid over the chain. "No, I was just being a Boy Scout. You know, be prepared?"

Jake prodded the Y-brace with his toe. "It looks like a medieval torture device."

Emily spared him a quick smile. "It may look like that, but pulling a breech calf without it is backbreaking." She reached into her first aid kit and grabbed a sealed package containing one sterile, shoulder-length, clear plastic glove. She tore it open and pulled the loose-fitting glove onto her right hand and up to cover her sleeve. She spilled the last of the iodine over her protected fingers. Sliding a loop of the sanitized chain over the baby's legs, she tightened them and turned to the brace.

Jake came around the other side of the placid animal. "Tell me where you want it."

Emily instructed Jake to hold the brace against Cowlick's back legs. She connected the chain to the lever on the brace. Emily pumped the lever up and down to take up the slack in the chain until it was taut. She stopped levering and turned to Jake. "Once I start, I've got to get it out of there fast. As its chest passes through the birth canal, its lungs are crushed. When the pressure comes off its lungs, the baby takes its first breath. Trouble is, when the chest delivers first, before its head, that breath is taken inside the mother. That means this little baby will be drowning."

"Let me pull the lever. I'm stronger."

Emily hesitated. "Your strength will help, but you've got to keep going even if it seems to be hurting Cowlick. I've heard cows make very distressed sounds. I've even seen a few fall down. When the going gets hardest, that's the exact moment you *can't* quit."

Jake met her eyes. "I won't quit."

She held his gaze, judging him. "Let's say a prayer before we start."

Jake nodded. "I'll say it."

Emily felt better after Jake's sincere request for help from God. "Okay, let's go."

Jake started hiking the lever. His muscles bulged under his T-shirt.

Emily knew a prayerful moment of gratitude. She would have been in trouble doing this alone. She watched the calf's hind legs emerge fully.

"Now's when it gets hard. Once its little rump is delivered it should be easy."

Jake worked the lever steadily, winding up one chain link at a time with the click of metal on metal.

Emily saw his lips moving and knew he'd kept up his prayers. She added her own. "Just a few more inches."

The lever stalled.

"It's not moving." Jake spoke through gritted teeth, leaning on the lever with all of his strength. His feet slipped a bit on the crackling straw.

Emily grabbed the calf's legs above the chain and pulled.

For a second, then two, nothing happened. Cowlick mooed in distress and twisted her head around, fighting the stanchion, to look over her shoulder.

Emily glanced up at Jake and saw regret over the pain he was causing. Then, with a sudden burst, the calf's little tail emerged and its hips, then it slid and landed on Emily like a wet sack of cement.

Rolling the soggy calf aside, Emily pulled the baby away from Cowlick's heels and knelt beside it. The calf wheezed. Emily grabbed a handful of clean straw and tickled its broad pink nose. "It's a little bull." Emily automatically checked. She glanced at Jake. "Grab his front leg. Like this." Emily bent one front leg double, pressing it against the calf's chest.

Jake was beside her instantly.

"Work his front leg up and down this way. It works like CPR. Maybe we can get the water out of him. Stephie, can you get the chains off his legs?"

They all three worked in silence. Emily got a few satisfactory sneezes out of the little bull, then he started fighting Jake.

Emily sat back on her heels. "Hold up."

Jake eased the leg out straight and sat back on his heels. "He doesn't seem too good."

"I think he's going to be okay." A soft crooning hum drew Emily's attention to Cowlick. Those gentle lowing noises were as natural to the little cow as giving milk. "Steph, let Cowlick out to meet her son." She pulled Jake away as the stanchion clicked open.

"You're a mommy now," Stephie sang.

Cowlick went immediately to her baby's side and started licking the white stripe down the center of its black face. The calf lifted its nose until he touched his mother's rough tongue with his own. Then, with a burst of energy, the baby shook his head vigorously and flailed his legs. Cowlick knocked him flat on his side with her tongue.

"She's hurting him." Jake rose from where he knelt on the barn floor.

Emily put a staying hand on his forearm. "Watch him liven up when she pushes him around. He pushes back. See." Emily pointed to the little one's uncoordinated efforts. "He's starting to use his muscles."

The baby sat up and resisted the seemingly careless ministrations of his mama. He leaned in to her licking, supporting himself against it.

Jake sank back on the floor, and Stephie's arms came around Emily's neck. The messy part of her work was done, so Emily stripped the plastic sleeve off her arm and tossed it into the iodine bucket. In silence, they watched the mother and calf.

Cowlick kept up a steady vibration from deep in her throat. The calf returned a juvenile imitation of the soothing song. The crooning settled into something spiritual.

Emily would have been content to sit there all night. She glanced at Jake to see if he was enjoying this as much as she was. A single tear rolled down his cheek.

Jake Hanson had learned to cry.

She smiled, then hoisted herself to her feet. "We need to get him up. He should have colostrum."

With a quick dash of his wrist across his eyes, Jake stood beside her ready to help. "What's colostrum?"

Emily's heart couldn't help but beat a little faster. He'd

made all the difference tonight. "Colostrum is the first milk the mother gives. It has a high concentration of protein and contains a natural antibiotic. The quicker we get some inside him the better. Especially since the fluid in his lungs can cause pneumonia."

"What do we do?"

"First let me get him on his feet." She could see that Jake thought it was too soon, but he nodded.

Emily pressed on the calf's hind quarters. The baby reacted by pulling its front legs more fully underneath it. Next it leaned forward on its knees, lurched on its back legs, and raised its hindquarters into the air. Emily waited for the little bull to get his balance, then, when she thought it was time, she wrapped her arms around his slimy belly and hoisted him onto all fours. He wavered on those long stilts for a precarious count of three before he dropped back to the floor.

Emily laughed. "Not bad for the first time, little guy. Let's go again."

The second time he didn't try at all. He just looked over his shoulder at Emily's prodding.

The third time, Jake helped lift and they had him on his feet for a split second before Cowlick knocked him over with her curious nose.

The fourth time he got up and stayed. He was so wobbly, standing upright looked like nothing short of a miracle. When he took his first staggered steps they all cheered, and the noise almost sent him back to the floor. Jake caught him. Emily then pushed him toward Cowlick's udder. Cowlick turned to follow the calf, which had the effect of moving her udder away from her hungry baby.

Emily shook her head in disgust. "Beef cattle are better at this. A lot of natural instincts have been bred out of Holsteins in an effort to get more milk."

"Why would getting more milk ruin a cow's instincts?"

Emily kept urging the calf toward the circling cow. "It's not that they tried to wreck the instincts, it's just that a dairy cow can live without them. A beef cow has her calf outside, with no people to help. The cow gives birth without trouble or she dies. The calf gets up without help and starts in eating or it dies. Survival of the fittest." Emily started urging the calf and Cowlick into a corner. "Although, I do check my cattle and I end up helping a few babies into the world every year. That's why I've got all this equipment. You know that buffalo herd near here?"

Jake looked away from Cowlick's baby. "You've mentioned it before."

"I was over there once when a buffalo cow gave birth. Compared to them even beef cattle are wimpy."

"How's that?"

"When I was there the herd was walking along, grazing, and Buffy pointed to one of them and said, 'Look, she's going to have a baby right now.'"

"The buffalo didn't head for some lonely spot?"

"Nope, they stay together. They know the herd is protection for them. The buffalo cow never stopped moving. The calf was born while she was walking and fell to the ground."

"Was it hurt?" Jake looked like he was ready to go have a stern talk with Buffy about protecting her herd better.

Emily smiled. "Not only was it not hurt, it bounced right onto its feet and chased after the mother."

Jake looked doubtful as he glanced at the wobbly Holstein calf.

"Buffy told me the mothers never look back. The calf catches up and eats on its own or it dies. She said with almost every birth she'd ever seen, the calf was on its feet and walking after its mother within sixty seconds."

"Wow, I'd like to see that." Jake almost looked like he'd come out of hiding.

It gave Emily hope. "Compare that to dairy farmers. They keep constant watch, especially on high-producing cows because the calves are worth sometimes thousands of dollars. Dairy farmers intervene in troubled births, like we just did. Cows that don't calf easily and don't have natural maternal instinct, *like standing still to let her calf eat*"—Emily aimed the last words at Cowlick and jammed her fists onto her hips as Cowlick nuzzled her baby, keeping her milk end far from her baby's mouth, and the calf standing there wobbling without a thought of eating—"still have babies that survive and grow up to reproduce, *no matter how dumb they are.*"

Emily pushed the baby again and Cowlick moved in the wrong direction. "Jake, stand on that side of her and keep her back end from moving away from me. Stephie, stay by her head and talk to her, distract her from licking the calf. If we can get the calf to eat once, they ought to get the idea."

Jake almost got shoved over for his trouble and Stephie wasn't as interesting to Cowlick as the calf, but finally the little bull latched on to supper.

His mama turned her head to watch him eat, now careful not to move her udder. Cowlick resumed her gentle lowing and licked along the baby's spine. With every drink, the calf gained strength and muscle control. His tiny tail began to twitch in time to his nursing.

Emily silently offered a prayer of thanks. She hadn't wanted Jake's first brush with the death of an animal to come so soon. It was a fact of life on the ranch, but he didn't have to learn that yet. With a satisfied sigh, she began picking up her equipment.

Jake took the heavy brace for her. "Let me carry it home for you."

"Leave it over by that wall for tonight. I don't have the energy to pack everything back home."

"Fine." Jake put the brace away. "What else do you need done?"

"Well, we need to treat his navel." Emily stooped and got her aerosol can of iodine out of the toolbox. She crouched beside the calf and sprayed under his stomach, careful to reach both sides. The sharp smell of iodine filled the barn as the bull's raw umbilical cord, hanging down under his belly, got painted bright purple from the spray.

"Then he needs a shot." She replaced the iodine can and extracted her hypodermic needle and the bottle of broad spectrum antibiotic. She poked the needle into the rubber cover on the bottle, pulled back the plunger on the syringe, and, giving Jake an apologetic grin, stabbed the poor little bull right in front of his tail, a few inches off to the side of his backbone.

"I know that must be necessary," Jake said through clenched teeth.

Emily patted him on the arm. "It is. New calves are so prone to infection, especially with such a difficult birth. I don't do it for my calves, but between the complicated birth and being a wimpy Holstein, I'm doing it as a precaution. I have to give him this one and a vitamin shot." She concentrated on the calf, not wanting to see Jake flinch when the needle stabbed in.

"If this was one of my calves, I'd tag his ear to identify him. Yours is going to be spared the piercing. Since you only have one calf, I think we'll be able to keep track of him." She grinned at Jake. "Let's move the two of them into the bigger stall at that end of the barn. Then we can go. I'd like to check him once more before bedtime, to make sure his lungs are clear, and maybe once around two."

In deference to Jake, Emily lured Cowlick into the stall with a bucket of grain without a single slap on her broad back. The calf trailed along unsteadily, chasing his escaping supper.

Emily and Stephie walked Jake back to his house, enjoying the pleasant evening and the chirping of grasshoppers. An owl hooted in the trees, and a warm breeze rustled the leaves and grass.

"Right now I'm really glad I didn't come out and stop you when you brought that tank of propane to the house." Jake looked down at his grubby clothes, then looked sideways at her with a naughty glint in his eye.

It took Emily a second to get it. "You saw me? You knew I was working on your water heater?"

He grinned. "Why should you be mad?"

"That bottle of gas was heavy. If you knew I was doing it you could have helped." She gave his filthy shoulder just the littlest shove with her equally filthy hand.

Jake laughed. "I'm the one who was getting modernized against my will." He bent and gave her the briefest possible kiss on the cheek. "See you later, in the maternity ward."

He went into the house, and she turned to her own home, still tingling from the drama and joy of the night and Jake's teasing, and maybe, just slightly, from that purely platonic kiss.

nineteen

If the calf had gotten sick, Jake knew he'd come out of hiding to find a cow emergency ward—if there was such a thing.

And Emily wouldn't respect spending thousands of dollars to save a calf worth a couple of hundred. It wasn't good business. To Jake's relief the calf was fine.

It was a good thing he was rich to begin with, because he couldn't make tough business choices about his animals' lives. He didn't mind. He could ranch for a long time before he used up all his money. Still, he was glad Emily didn't have to know.

He let the calf have all the milk it wanted and still got a gallon from Cowlick every morning and night. It was more than Jake, the Johannsons, and the kittens could drink, so they were throwing the extra away.

Stephie surprised him by loving to milk. As soon as Emily was satisfied that Cowlick wouldn't kick, she agreed to turn the chore over to her little sister.

Jake helped with the haying and couldn't believe the hard work involved. "You throw bales by yourself?"

Emily shrugged and gave him an evil grin. "Normally I'd hire a couple of high school boys to help. But I can't because they'd find out about you. So you get to take up the slack."

Jake looked at her as she climbed down from the hayrack. She stopped the tractor every dozen or so bales and pretended to help him straighten the load, but the load was perfectly straight. She was just giving him a break. Good thing, hoisting seventy-five-pound bales continuously for four hours almost killed him.

He ached for a week. The heavy lifting wakened a white-knight reflex and made him fiercely glad he could help. Her

130

gratitude rang in his ears until he cherished every one of his stiff muscles.

Around the end of July, Emily announced the chickens were old enough to eat. It sent Jake into a tailspin. He endured several days of Emily's abuse before he noticed she wasn't chasing any of them down either.

At lunch one day—fried chicken from the grocery store—Jake braced her about it. "You don't want to eat those chickens any more than I do."

Emily got really busy dishing up slices of the first tomatoes of the summer and didn't look him in the eye. "It's not that I mind eating them. . .much." She looked up, her eyes wide. "I just don't want to get them ready to eat."

Stephie made a gagging noise, then went back to gobbling down the coleslaw they'd made from the cabbage in the garden.

Jake scowled at Emily. "You mean you can't look into their trusting little eyes and chop their heads off?" Jake would never go after one of his very own chickens with an ax.

Near as he could tell, Emily was suddenly fascinated by the task of buttering her corn on the cob. "It's not like I *couldn't* do it. I could. If I had to."

"You've been torturing me for days."

She flung her arms wide. "It's not like we're starving."

So the chickens were spared.

About that time, Jake discovered chickens were stupid. They would not stay in their pen. Despite constant patching, they always found a way out. He found droppings all over, in extremely unpleasant ways.

Then they began to vanish. Jake knew because Emily had ordered him to count his chickens every morning.

He had about forty left. "What is going on? There were fifty chickens when you brought them home."

"Hawks or owls probably. It's just a hazard that goes along with raising chickens."

Jake planted his fists on his hips. "Well if they're going to be eaten anyway, it seems like we ought to get to eat them."

"Ain't that the truth." Emily didn't go for the ax, and Jake couldn't, so the hawks were living large.

Next the dumb clucks all started picking on one chicken. To save it, Jake built it a separate yard. Then the birds simply chose another of their kind to harass.

When he had seven separate pens scattered around his yard, he could have killed a few leghorns, fried them up, and savored every bite. When the blasted birds discovered his fledgling garden and cleared out every speck of green, he entered a martyr zone.

The end came when they started on Emily's garden. The rancher in her rediscovered itself and Jake didn't even bat an eye when she announced the high-tech compromise of taking the roosters, about half the dwindling flock, to the local meat locker to be butchered. It wasn't what a pioneer would have done, but having Emily's freezer stuffed with chicken was one modern compromise Jake decided he liked.

Emily had to drive miles out of her way to get to his place, but she showed up with a stack of wooden crates in her truck late one night while the chickens were roosting for the night in the chicken house. She quietly entered the small building, then caught the unsuspecting roosters by the legs. They squawked and flapped, but the other chickens stayed put as their brethren got hauled away. Emily tucked them in the crates and it took a few trips before Jake waded in and started helping.

As they took away the last of the roosters, Jake remembered his poor pumpkins plants. "The hens are eating the garden, too. Let's throw them in." Jake felt like he'd just imposed the death penalty on his friends. Of course he was royally sick of his friends, so he found he could live with it.

"Good call." Emily started snagging the rest of them. "Eggs are cheap."

❧

Jake had rediscovered his love of farming when Stephie came

running into his house one Sunday evening, shortly after Jake had come home from supper and settled in to study the Bible Emily had given him. Emily brought him the bulletin from church every week and gave him a few notes about the sermon. He spent time daily in prayer and Bible study, but on Sunday nights he made it a point to worship.

"I can't find Cowlick."

"I checked her just before I came over to your place to eat." Jake grabbed a jacket and followed Stephie outside in the drizzle. His yard was soaked from a weekend of heavy rains. Emily had been smiling ever since the downpour started Friday night, saying a heavy rain in July made all the difference in her third cutting hay crop. Jake saw Cowlick's tracks leaving the cow yard through that stupid, knocked-down gate. Why hadn't he gotten it wired up more solidly?

"I'll go after her. You go get Emily, okay?"

Stephie nodded and ran for her big sister. The two of them caught up with him coming back from the spot where Cowlick had gone to have her baby. "I went all the way to the edge of the pasture. She's not there."

Emily looked grim. "I'd better get my pickup. No sense ruining your Jeep on this rutted field."

Emily was a while driving over because of the circuitous route she had to take around the creek, but she finally arrived. Jake and Stephie came out of the barn where they'd gone to avoid the rain, and climbed in. The rain had slowed to a sprinkle, but the pasture was soft.

They swung around a five-mile stretch of land between Jake's place and the nearest highway.

"We're running out of places to look." Emily wrestled the truck over the muddy, rutted pastureland.

Stephie screamed. "I see the calf." She pointed to a spot right beside the wooded creek. The calf stood inches from the bank.

Emily pulled to a stop. They jumped out and went to the calf, expecting to see Cowlick in the woods, but when Jake stepped past the first tree, the ground, mushy from rain, broke off under his feet.

Emily grabbed him as he stumbled backward from the edge or he'd have fallen into the creek. "Why isn't that fenced?"

"Because cows are instinctively smart enough to stay away from the edge," Emily answered.

Jake's throat went dry. "Didn't you say dairy cattle had the instincts bred out of them?"

twenty

"That calf isn't standing here for his health." Emily looked at the muddy bank. The calf bawled at the creek.

Jake shook his head as he ran one hand into his damp hair.

"I'm going to have to go down there." Emily stood in the drizzling rain, glaring at that cold muddy bank. She thought of the hot supper she'd just slid off the stove and her clean, comfortable kitchen. But ranchers learn about hard work at a young age.

"All right, you guys hold on to the calf. Don't let it loose or it might fall in next." Emily took two steps.

Jake grabbed her arm. "I'll do it."

Emily smiled. "You're not wearing overshoes."

He glanced at his feet sheepishly.

"There's still enough light if we hurry. Let go." She jerked her arm.

His jaw worked, then he released her.

Dusk gathered in the gloomy sky as Emily, clinging to passing branches, slipped and slid and ran and mostly fell to the bottom of the bank. The leaves overhead dripped with misting rain. Bending under branches, Emily slogged through the deep mud that bordered the meandering rivulet of creek water. She was ready to turn and scout the other direction when she saw an unusually smooth stretch of mud.

Then the mud blinked.

Emily's stomach twisted as she realized Cowlick was lying on her side, coated with mud and sunk in until she hardly made a bump on the muddy surface. Her head was coated and her nose. She couldn't be alive.

Then that eye blinked again.

Emily waded in. Mud flowed over the tops of her boots. She got to Cowlick's head and, with a sucking sound, lifted. Emily sank to her knees as she wiped out Cowlick's nose with the sleeve of her denim jacket. Then she tore the jacket off and used every inch of it to clear Cowlick's air passages.

Emily twisted herself around until she sat in the mud under Cowlick's head. "Jake, can you hear me?" The top of the creek bank seemed a million miles away.

"Yeah, I'm here. You want me to come down?" His voice, clearly audible, had to be twenty feet straight above her head. How were they ever going to get Cowlick up that hill?

"No, I found her but I can't get her out. We're going to. . ." Emily didn't know if Jake could do everything, but she couldn't leave Cowlick. "This is gonna get complicated."

"Tell me." His voice was like a weight lifting off Emily. She had appreciated all he did to make her life easier through this summer, but until this minute she didn't realize how alone she'd been. "Go to my place. The tractor we bale with—"

"The Thirty-Twenty International?"

He really did know what to do. "Yeah, you have to take the baler off and hook up the blade."

"The yellow one in your machine shed?"

"That's right. You know how to attach it, right?"

"Does it have those quick attaching clamps like the baler?"

"Yes, it's the same. Bring it." The mud oozed higher on Emily's body. "And bring all the log chain you can find. There's some in all four tractors, one in the toolbox in my truck, and two lengths in the barn. We're going to need enough to stretch from up there to Cowlick, and we can't get the tractor too close to the edge."

There was an extended moment of silence.

"I'll come down. You go do all this." He sounded like he hated to leave her.

She appreciated that. "Hurry up, hotshot. I'm taking a mud bath down here and it's not the thrill you might expect."

"Be right back. Let's go, Stephie."

The truck's engine started up and quickly faded into the distance. The calf bawled and Emily wished she'd thought to tell them to take the calf. The way this night was going, the calf would fall over the edge next, although the little guy had shown more sense than his mother so far.

It was fully dark now. At first she just sat and absorbed how alone she and Cowlick were. Except for the mud and the cold rain that dripped through the tree and down her neck, it wasn't a bad feeling.

The night closed in around Emily. Crickets chirping and frogs croaking began to take on a menacing edge. Hours seemed to pass as she sat surrounded by the night. She spent a nice chunk of it in prayer. For strength to get this cow out of the creek. And thanking God that they'd found her alive.

When she heard the roar of her tractor, Emily breathed a sigh of relief.

The motor cut back to a lower growl and the cab door slammed. "What now?" Jake's voice gave her a boost of energy.

"Link the chains and lower them. We'll use them to get Cowlick unstuck first. We have to get her out of this mudhole. There's a more gradual slope down a few feet that if we cut it down with the blade, once she's unstuck and we get her up, she might be able to climb out."

Emily heard the clinking of the heavy chain and watched for the black chain on the black ground in the black night. When she finally spotted it, Emily pulled out from under Cowlick with some difficulty. Cowlick, exhausted, dropped her head in the mud.

Emily grabbed the chain, then scrambled around to Cowlick's belly. Burrowing her arms under the little cow, Emily shoved the chain under her belly right behind the cow's front legs.

"Let me lift her." Jake's deep voice sounded inches behind her.

Emily squeaked with fright. Then his strong hands joined

hers as he knelt beside her in the muck, sliding the chain further. Cowlick lurched, struggling to free herself. Emily's hands skidded. She landed face first on Cowlick's belly. She knocked into Jake, who lost his footing and tipped sideways into the mud up to his shoulder on the left side.

Emily pulled herself up as Jake scrambled back to his knees. Swiping the sludge off her face, Emily shook her hands, then looked grimly at her mud-soaked neighbor. Her eyes had adjusted to the dark enough to see the left half of his face was coated with mud.

"You know, Jake, animals get in trouble more often than you'd think. You sacrifice meals and sleep and your body to take care of them. A rancher does that because that's what a rancher does."

Jake angled his body toward her, but his knees were so deep in the mud they didn't move. "Are you saying a rancher's gotta do what a rancher's gotta do?" Jake asked sardonically.

Emily smiled, but the mud on her face had started to harden so she doubted if her lips actually curved up. "The point is, this moment, right here, right now, this is what ranching is really like."

Jake gave an unintelligible grunt that matched Emily's mood pretty well. "This moment, right here, right now, I'm glad I came to ranching later in life. I'll always be happy to know I missed thirty years of it." He went back to work on the log chain.

Finally, they got it fastened.

"You go up and drive," Jake offered. "I'll push."

Emily nodded, not sure she had the energy to climb the steep bank but sure she didn't match Jake in brute strength. His muscle would ease the strain on Cowlick when the tractor pulled on her. "Hold her head out of the mud. She's drowning."

Jake was already doing it.

Emily dragged herself out of the mudhole and headed up.

She crawled up the bank on her hands and knees.

"Emily, you're muddy." Stephie stood hugging the baby calf.

Emily thought that summed it up nicely. "You listen to Jake. I won't be able to hear him over the tractor."

"Okay." Stephie let go of the little bull.

"You get that, Jake?" Emily yelled.

"Got it."

Emily kept yelling at the disembodied voice in the darkness. "We'll pull her free, then figure out how to get her up! Yell when she's loose!"

"Stephie"—Emily turned to her little sister—"when Jake yells, run in front of the tractor and wave your arms and yell your head off. But be careful. Stay away from the tractor and get out front where my headlights can find you. I'll be going really slow. Make a big motion like this." Emily raised both hands over her head and crossed them at the wrist, then lowered them straight out at her sides. "Got it?"

Stephie imitated the motion.

"Don't get close to the tractor." Emily picked up the chain, attached it to the back of the tractor, and scaled the high steps. She put the big machine in gear, increased the torque to a roar, and eased the tractor forward. Seconds after she started, Stephie dashed forward, shouting and waving frantically. Emily locked the brake and jumped back to the ground. She slipped and slid and ran and mostly fell down the bank and slogged to Jake's side.

Cowlick refused to stand.

"I'm going to use the blade to knock out a slope. Right over there." Emily pointed to the place she'd just come down. "Stay with her."

"You've already been up and down that bank four times. I'll climb out."

Emily, already halfway up the slope, yelled, "I'm not strong enough to stop her if she starts sliding back into the mud!"

Emily gave up ten seconds after she started. The creek bank

was too unstable to risk getting her tractor that close. "Jake, has she stood up yet?"

"No, she won't even try." His deep voice seemed disembodied, like the creek was speaking to her.

"Okay, we're going to have to pull her up with the chain."

"It's too hard on her!" Jake yelled. "You'll kill her!"

"I don't know how else to do it." Grimly worried about the cow, Emily didn't wait for an answer. She backed the tractor up to the chain and reattached it.

"Stephie, signal just like before if Jake wanted the tractor stopped." Her jaw clenched, Emily pulled slowly away from the bank.

At last, Stephie charged in front of the tractor, waving.

Emily jumped to the ground.

"We got her up, Emily!" Stephie yelled.

Emily hurried to Cowlick's side. Jake was just getting to the top of the bank. Cowlick, lying out flat on the ground, didn't even react as they unhooked the chain. The baby calf bawled and bunted at his mother. Cowlick's legs jerked and she lifted her head, but she didn't try to get up.

"We're just going to have to let her rest." Emily patted the cow's muddy side. "Let's get some feed and water for her. If we can get her to eat, she may be okay in the morning."

They rode back in the overcrowded tractor cab. Emily got a small bucket of corn and some water. The mud was dry and flaking off in big chunks. She drove out to the spot where they had left Cowlick, her truck's windshield wipers swiping at the drizzling rain.

Jake, on the passenger's side, reached across Stephie to grip Emily's arm. "She's gone."

"That means she got up." Emily smiled, and the mud on her face cracked. "She'll live."

Jake sagged against the seat. He hadn't worried out loud about Cowlick, but Emily knew he loved the little cow.

"Let's see where she's gotten to." Emily drove along the

creek. When she was sure Cowlick couldn't have come this far, she swung her truck around. Her headlights fell broadside on Cowlick, calmly grazing right beside the creek. The headlights startled her and she jumped.

Emily watched in horror as Cowlick disappeared over the edge of the creek bank. The three of them sat in stunned silence for what seemed like an eternity.

At last, Emily turned to Jake. "Go get the tractor and the log chains. I'll make sure she isn't drowning." She stepped out of the truck. "And this time, take the calf back and lock it in the barn." Without a backward glance, she dropped over the edge of the bank and they repeated everything.

When they got Cowlick up, Emily refused to believe her injured act and insisted the cow get to her feet.

Emily walked behind Cowlick and herded her all the way back to the barn. Jake drove in on the tractor with Stephie, half asleep, squashed beside him.

It was eleven thirty when Emily finished triple-wiring the faulty gate panel. Jake, Stephie, and Emily stood in the sullen rain and stared at the mud-caked cow eating placidly out of her feed bunk while her baby nursed.

Emily tugged her gloves off. "Jake?" she said quietly.

"Hmmm?" Jake looked away from Cowlick.

"I've been ranching, really all my life. Twenty-four years." Half a pound of mud broke off her gloves and fell to the ground. Stephie, still mostly clean but drenched, took a step away from her big sister.

Jake nodded. "That's a long time."

"It's a quarter of a century." She started to tuck her gloves behind her belt, then stopped. "I've seen a lot. Handled thousands of cows. In all circumstances. In all weather."

Jake looked up at the drizzle that had soaked them all to the bone. "Your point?"

"I have one," Emily said.

Jake stood silently.

"In all those years. . ." Emily pounded her ruined leather work gloves—expensive suckers, fifteen dollars a pair—against her leg. "In all those years," she repeated ominously, "that"—she jabbed her gloves at Cowlick—"is the stupidest cow I have ever seen."

Jake just nodded his head.

Emily and Stephie headed for home.

twenty-one

The mud bath was the clincher for Jake.

He quit feeling like he had anything to prove. He was a rancher now, or maybe a farmer. He might need more cows and a lot more land to qualify for a ranch. Still, this was the Black Hills. Out here everyone ranched. So why not him?

He gave up his desire to be a pioneer. He agreed to let Emily use her name to get his electricity turned on, and he agreed to get new kitchen appliances. Intimidated by the unfamiliar job of buying a stove and refrigerator, he begged Emily and Stephie to go with him.

"You can't buy appliances in Cold Creek. Hot Springs has a hardware store that sells some, but we'll see someone we know there and I'll have to explain who you are."

He waved away her concern. For some reason it seemed awfully important to take Emily along. "What's the big deal? Hi, I'm Emily's cousin." He put tons of sincerity in his voice.

"That's excellent. You're a wonderful liar. You must be very proud," Emily said dryly. "The trouble is everyone knows I don't have any cousins around here. They'd immediately ask"—Emily raised the pitch of her voice to imitate a nosy old lady—" 'Are you a cousin on Emily's mother's side or her father's side?' "Her voice returned to normal. "Then they'd want to know whose boy you are."

"Boy?"

"Sorry, but if you're my cousin, then you're somebody's child. Anyone who knows me knows my dad has two older brothers and my mom has one sister. They'd want to know about—"

"Okay, I get it." He hesitated, torn between wanting her help and wanting to keep his secret. He snapped his fingers. "We'll just go farther."

"I guess we could go to Rapid City. But it's a long ways. Just go alone to Hot Springs. Being with me is the problem."

"I really think I need some help with the stove and refrigerator." He was disgusted with himself for deliberately trying to sound pathetic, especially when it worked. He supposed that meant he wasn't faking. He really *was* pathetic.

"Okay, we'll do Rapid City. It will have everything we need, a two-hour drive."

"I'm up for that. Maybe we can take Stephie to a movie or something, go to a nice restaurant for lunch. Let's go in the morning, after milking. We can be home for evening chores."

Emily nodded her head. "All right. But it's probably a mistake. We might see people I know in Rapid City, too. I'm just trying to protect your secret."

"I appreciate that." Jake smiled at her. "You haven't ever told anyone, have you? I can't believe that."

"I gave you my word." Emily crossed her arms.

"Yes, you did. I'm learning that really means something. I'm learning a lot of things out here."

"How about no?"

"No? What are you talking about? Don't you want to help me buy the appliances?"

"Have you learned to say no? Are you ready to face your old life?"

She'd told him to learn to laugh, and to cry, and to say no. Well, he'd never laughed so much in his life. And he'd shed a few tears of joy over the survival of his baby calf. But Emily didn't really understand what he had to contend with at Hanson and Coltrain. How could he turn his back on people in such dreadful need?

He tried not to think about it, but that night the anticipation over the trip kept him awake. He, who had jetted to his ski lodge in Aspen and owned a condo in Chicago, places he'd inherited from his wealthy father, was excited over a cookstove.

His thoughts chased in circles. People were dying somewhere in the world, right now, and he could help save them. What about those heavy hay bales? He was needed here.

He wanted to stay. He wanted his animals and his garden. He wanted Stephie holding his hand, her eyes full of trust. He wanted to work alongside Emily for the rest of his life.

He wanted Emily.

Jake's hands started shaking. Being part of a family was like stepping into pure darkness and hoping the black didn't hide a bottomless pit. Only now, as he lay in bed, did he realize how terrified he was of taking this risk. He prayed for the courage to choose love; he prayed for God to lead him. But how could God want Jake to turn his back on people suffering, bleeding, dying?

When he'd walked in on Tish with another man, well, he'd been disgusted, but he'd known what kind of woman she was. That was one of the reasons he'd kept company with her, and there'd never been a chance he'd love Tish.

Emily was different. She had the power to hurt him. No one, not his mother or father, no girlfriend, had ever cared enough about him to stay. He had no control over his parents, except the confused feeling that if he'd been more lovable somehow maybe they'd have loved him. But the girlfriends—he'd had very few because his job made him leave town suddenly and for extended periods of time.

It came to him in a rush. He wanted to stand next to Emily, holding her hand, as she gave birth to their child. Then, over the joyous image, washed visions of lives lost because he was too late evacuating a building.

He sank back onto his mattress. For all his doubts he was sure of two things: He had to deal with Hanson and Coltrain, and he had no peace about abandoning his work. If he left here to face Sid Coltrain and sever his ties to his old life, he might never be back. He knew he still hadn't learned to say no.

Until he did, he and Emily could never be together.

twenty-two

"I've got him." Sid slammed the phone down.

"You're sure?" Tish came out looking artfully disheveled.

"I've got a flight out of O'Hare in two hours and a helicopter on standby in Rapid City. Wear that red dress." *It took her two hours to get that casual look*, Sid thought with a sneer.

"But how will you get him to come back?" Tish's crimson nails fluffed her blond curls, looking like blood dripping through her hair.

"Let me call the office. There have to be orphans dying somewhere." He listened a few minutes, then rapped some orders into the phone and slammed down the receiver.

"Move it, Tish. There's a limo waiting out front to take us to the airport."

&

Emily might as well have ridden to town with Cowlick in the seat beside her. The little cow would have had more to say. An occasional moo. . .something.

Yesterday he had begged her to go along, as if buying a stove was so difficult. Now he barely looked at them.

Stephie kept patting him on the knee and trying to talk to him. The ride to Rapid City would have been accomplished in total silence if it hadn't been for Stephie. She was probably in seventh heaven, talking to her heart's content.

Emily's stomach twisted because the only thing that could be bothering Jake this much was leaving.

Maybe he was fighting it now, but he would leave. He had too much honor to hide for long. When he'd healed, he'd return to his old life. She'd known it from the first. But knowing hadn't protected Emily's heart.

146

Once the city finally came into sight, they drove straight to the mall and she led the way inside. She snagged the first employee she found and said, "Give me the cheapest stove and refrigerator you've got."

The heavyset man arched his eyebrows. "Gas or electric?"

"Doesn't matter." Emily thought she must have looked determined because he didn't try to talk her up to something better.

Jake paid with a wad of hundreds.

Their big day out was over by eleven o'clock. Emily drove straight to Jake's house. She didn't bother with the field roads, and even when they passed someone she knew, she never warned him to keep his head down. She helped him unload the stove and refrigerator, and hook them up. The gas flame jumped to life with a quiet whoosh, then Stephie ran out to see the calf.

"You want to tell me what's going on?" Emily switched off the flame with a sharp click, then faced Jake. Crossing her arms, she leaned against the stove.

Jake sank onto a kitchen chair and looked up. It was the first time he'd made eye contact all morning. "I did a lot of thinking last night."

"Come to any decisions?"

"I don't want to go." Suddenly his eyes, so dull all morning, blazed with a fire that seemed to come straight from his soul. "I don't want to leave you."

He erupted out of the chair, sending it sliding backward until it crashed against a wall and toppled over with a bang. He pulled her into his arms.

Emily wrapped her arms around him, wanting to cling, knowing it would do no good. Her face pressed against his chest, she said, "You don't want to go. But you have to. I understand."

Jake's hand slid into her hair, left loose for the trip to the city. "How can you understand when I don't?" He tilted her face up so she had to look at him.

"It's not so hard to understand. You don't have anything to offer me as long as you're running."

"It's because of you I've found the courage to go back. I want to promise I'll return, but. . ." His voice faltered.

Just when she was sure she couldn't love him any more than she already did, she loved him for not making a promise he couldn't keep. "When will you go?"

"Soon, but I'm not leaving without telling you what you mean to me. Emily, I—"

The house shook. Dirt hit the kitchen window and the glass rattled against the sill. Stephie must not have pulled the back door all the way shut because it flew open and banged against the wall.

Emily looked out the window. A helicopter landed on Jake's pumpkin patch.

twenty-three

Jake stepped to the back door. Dirt blew in with stinging force.

Emily saw the door of the helicopter open and a dark-suited man stepped out, followed by a woman dressed in red.

"Sid." Jake sounded as if he were uttering profanity.

Emily waited to hear the woman's name, but Jake stormed out, slamming the door behind him. Emily watched Jake's arms flail. The other man appeared to be completely calm.

She didn't take her eyes off the confrontation until the door opened, admitting the lady in red Emily had seen emerge along with Sid. Emily looked at the silky dress, tight enough to have been spray painted on, short enough to wade through the worst mudhole without damage, low-cut enough to nurse a baby while barely stretching the neckline. She glanced down at her own attire—her best T-shirt and blue jeans. She noticed a greasy smear on her shirt that must have rubbed off the stove as they'd hauled it in.

The woman's blond hair was a perfect mass of curls, miraculously undisturbed by the rotor wind. Her makeup was flawless, her lips the same shade of red as her dress, shoes, and nails. Long claws reached for Emily.

It took Emily too long to realize she was being offered a handshake. By the time she figured it out, she felt like a bumpkin.

"I'm Tish. I'm Jake's fiancée. And you are. . . ?"

The announcement hit Emily like a blow. She managed an awkward shake. "I'm Emily Johannson."

"It's always nice to meet the woman keeping Jake. . .happy."

The comment was so loaded it left Emily speechless.

"He has to get away once in a while. Sid and I understand."

"He. . .he's done this before?" Something wasn't right. Emily looked into golden brown eyes that gleamed like a predator's.

"He works in a terribly high-pressure job. We indulge him if we can, but eventually he has to come home." The bombshell smiled kindly, but the kindness didn't reach those eyes.

Emily remained silent. There seemed to be no point. Whatever game these three were playing, she was sitting in the stands.

"I hope you understand that you have to let him go. He was honest with you I hope." Pity oozed through Tish's scarlet lips.

Emily couldn't stand another syllable. "Jake's always been honest with me."

"It's not the first time he's taken a break from our relationship." A glint of pity in Tish's eyes humiliated Emily. "But in the end he's mine." Tish raised her hand again and, as she was meant to, Emily noticed a huge diamond on Tish's hand.

All she knew about Jake told Emily this was a lie.

Stephie came in crying, her hair flying loose from her braids. "I've got dirt in my eyes."

Emily guided Stephie to the bathroom, glad to escape. She was done rinsing Stephie's eyes with cool water when Jake came in. He opened the door to the little refuge Emily had found.

"I've got to go."

Emily knew no amount of crying or begging would sway him, not that she would ever demean herself by doing that. She didn't know what to say, so she said nothing.

Stephie didn't fling herself into his arms. Instead she backed against Emily. "I'll miss you."

Emily rested her hand on Stephie's head and her little sister turned her face into Emily's stomach.

"Something's happened, hasn't it?" Whatever she meant to him, it wasn't enough to make him stay.

"There's been a typhoon in the Philippines. Tens of thousands of people are homeless. There's no water." Jake ran a hand into his hair and Emily realized he'd never gotten a haircut since he arrived. The bleak look that had faded from his eyes was back and the lines around his mouth were deep, pulling his lips downward. It was like he'd lost all the peace of mind he'd found after one quick meeting with his business partner.

Emily's heart ached for him.

"They're calling in every man in the country who can help with the job."

"Jake, I want you to know I—"

Tish soundlessly stepped into the doorway behind Jake.

"You what?" Hope glowed in Jake's eyes. But Emily couldn't say what was in her heart in front of Tish.

"I. . .understand."

He leaned forward, and for a moment she thought she saw promises in his eyes. She thought he would take her in his arms and kiss her and say he'd be back.

But instead he reached one hand out and rested it in Stephie's hair. "Take care of Lucky for me, okay?"

Stephie nodded. "We'll take care of everything."

Jake left his hand on Stephie's head like a benediction. Then he shared a final look of longing with Emily. He turned and swept past Tish. Tish gave Emily a single triumphant smirk and flounced away.

Emily didn't come out of the bathroom until she heard the roar of the helicopter die in the distance.

"Is Jake coming back, Emily?"

Emily struggled to be brave for Stephie. "I don't know."

She wondered if it would be okay to talk to Helen Murray now. She'd wait until Jake gave her permission. If that meant waiting forever, then so be it.

Stephie squeezed Emily's hand. "You liked him a lot, didn't you?"

"Yeah." She didn't know what else to say. "He was fun to have around."

Stephie, with the resignation in her voice of someone who had lived a great many years, said, "When you weren't saving his life."

They walked home, holding hands, Lucky dancing at their heels.

twenty-four

A month and no word.

No phone calls, nothing. No disaster took this long to clean up. He had to be home. But he wasn't here, so that meant that this wasn't home. He had returned to Chicago and his old life.

Emily tried to figure out how she could have found him so irresistible. The reason, when it finally came to her, was so simple it was a miracle she hadn't thought of it sooner.

She loved him.

She loved him in a way that she had never known existed. She loved him like he was the other half of herself, just as her father had loved her mother, and her father had died from a broken heart. Emily knew she was too young and strong, and too desperately needed by Stephie, to let herself curl up and die. So she just died inside.

She went to church but she couldn't stand to visit, not even with Buffy, who had always been so friendly. Stephie rode to Sunday school with the Murrays, Emily slipped in late and hurried away. Stephie seemed to understand and cooperated. Or maybe Stephie was just heartbroken, too.

Emily's only consolation was that Jake didn't know how she felt. He and Tish probably laughed over the little country hick that adored him. It made her sick to think about Jake with that beautiful woman. How many times had she worn her ratty work boots and old jeans? She remembered Tish's sleek perfection and compared it to herself, tossing bales, soaked with sweat.

It was Saturday, so Stephie was around somewhere, running in the woods probably. School had started up, so most of Emily's days stretched long and silent. Emily did her best during the day to work and nurture her anger, but the nights were torture.

She dreamed of him. She stayed up late working, trying to avoid the memory. When she did sleep, she woke often with his name on her lips, and more sleep was impossible. Instead of lying in bed, torturing herself, she'd get up and start her day before sunrise.

She'd never said the words, but she'd loved him, maybe from the first day.

She wondered if he could even remember her name.

She was in her second week of building a rock garden on the side of the hill between her house and the woods that led to Jake's. They had an old rock pile overgrown with weeds. For years her father had tossed stones he dug up in the fields in the same spot. It was about a hundred yards down the hill from her new landscaping project. She was well on her way toward using up the whole collection. The backbreaking labor and the brutally aching muscles fit Emily's mood perfectly.

Today, with a blazing sun she would have ridiculed Jake for working under, she rolled a huge slab of limestone up the last few feet of the slope. On her knees, throwing every ounce of her strength into each inch of progress she gained, she counted off the days Jake had been gone. She'd gotten up to thirty-four days and started counting again. . .twice.

Someone touched her on the shoulder. With a startled twist, Emily jumped to her feet and almost fell over.

Helen Murray stood behind her, smiling. "Emily, I love what you're doing here. It's going to be beautiful."

Emily steadied herself, her heart slamming in her chest.

Helen gasped as she got a good look at Emily. "What's wrong? Are you sick?" Helen's eyes moved up and down Emily's body, pausing for a long time on her face.

"No, you just startled me." With one look at Helen's expression, Emily knew her neighbor wasn't asking about her jumpiness.

"You don't look well. You've lost weight. How hard have you been working on this?" Suddenly Helen started looking around the whole place.

There wasn't a weed anywhere. The fence and buildings had been painted. The vegetable garden and flower beds were picture perfect.

"Emily, are you getting ready for something? The place looks wonderful." Helen's wise eyes went back to Emily's face.

"I can't talk about it." Then Emily started crying. She covered her mouth with the back of one grubby hand to hold back the sobs.

Helen held Emily's eyes, then, with a sad smile, she brushed several sweat-soaked hairs off Emily's forehead, tucking them gently behind one ear. "Then it must be a man."

Emily shrugged her shaking shoulders and wearily nodded.

"It might help to tell me." Helen's work-roughened hand rested on Emily's shoulder and urged her down onto the rock Emily had been pushing.

"It might," she murmured through her tears.

"Where's Stephie, honey?"

"She's playing in the woods."

"You want me to call Carl and have him come and get her? We could talk in private then. For as long as you need to."

Emily shrugged again. She just didn't know what to do anymore. She sat for a long time, shedding all of her long overdue tears as Helen patted her back and made all the perfect sounds of comfort mothers know so well. When Emily's tears finally ended, Helen took her arm and guided her toward the house.

"I haven't heard from you all summer. I've tried to call a dozen times." Helen looked around the groomed yard. "Guess you've been outside, huh?"

Emily nodded.

They entered the house and Helen paused. The kitchen gleamed like it had been scrubbed by Mr. Clean on steroids. "You've been working inside some, too."

Emily swiped a few straggling tears away.

"When's the last time you ate?"

She'd been expecting some demand for a confession. The

mention of food caught her off guard. "Breakfast."

"What time?"

"Five, I guess." Emily wished she'd answered differently when Helen's lips formed a grim line.

"It's past three. Did you feed Stephie dinner?"

"I fed her." For the first time Emily found a little spirit. "She had a good meal. I'm taking care of her."

"Just not yourself," Helen said.

Emily's weak show of self-defense evaporated.

"Wash your hands, young lady. Then sit. You can talk while I fix you something, and then you can eat while I fix your problems." Helen sounded stern but she had a generous smile.

Helen's confidence made Emily wonder if maybe her problems could be fixed. So Emily talked while Helen cooked.

"He lived up there all that time and no one knew? That's amazing."

"He lived there two weeks before I discovered him. Pretty weird, huh?"

"If it makes you feel better, you can call him weird," Helen said with mock seriousness.

"To be honest, it does a little." Emily felt a trace of waspishness.

Helen laughed. "Are you sure he's gone for good?"

"I don't know." Emily must have used up all of her tears, because the question broke her heart but her eyes remained dry. "I guess. Wouldn't he have called if he was coming back?"

"You've had no calls, no letters?"

Emily shook her head.

"Have you tried to call him?"

"No! And I'm not going to!" Emily shouted. "What would I say? 'Please come back anytime you're bored'?" It felt good to shout.

Helen put an omelet in front of her.

The anger gave Emily an appetite and made her think of her stomach instead of her heart. And not thinking of her heart gave her spare brain space to think of her little sister. "Stephie's been gone too long. I should go check on her."

"Eat first. Stephie's fine."

Emily started on the omelet and it tasted like sawdust, like everything else she'd eaten for a month. Sawdust. She couldn't think about sawdust without thinking about her first meeting with Jake. His chest had been sprinkled with. . .

"Stop daydreaming. Forget about him until you finish your food."

Emily had heard that voice before. It was the one Helen used to get her children to eat. It worked; she took another bite.

"I think you should try to find him." Helen gave her head a firm jerk and set her spare chins to wobbling.

Emily had just swallowed or she would have choked. She dropped her fork onto her plate with a clatter. "How could a phone call be anything but pathetic?"

"I'll call him right now if you don't finish your eggs."

Helen was a master at getting kids to eat, but Emily had a feeling broken hearts were outside her experience. Emily picked up her fork and forced another bite. "I don't have a phone number. I couldn't call him anyway."

"You just told me he works for Hanson and Coltrain in Chicago. You could find him with two phone calls. And you don't have to be pathetic. In fact, I'll stand beside you and thunk you on the head if you start sounding the least bit pitiful. What harm is there in an acquaintance calling to say hi? Or you could say you thought he'd like to know how his calf was doing. If you mean nothing to him, he won't think that's so strange. You know, he may have even tried to call. I've been phoning all month."

"I can't do it. He'll know how much I miss him. It's too humiliating."

"Honestly, Emily, can you feel any worse?" Helen waited for an answer.

Emily silently took another bite of food under Helen's watchful gaze. The thought of feeling even more miserable was unbearable.

"You know what I think? I think you'd feel better. If he is nasty to you, it will help you realize what a rat he is. Right now all you have are good memories and the big hero flying off into the sunset. You left too much unsettled. At least if he brushes you off, you'll get mad. Doesn't that make sense?"

Emily reached for more omelet and was surprised to find it gone. The food and Helen's solid support gave her a little stiffness in her spaghetti spine. "Some sense, I guess."

"So what do you say? Let's get the big dumb creep on the phone and see what he has to say for himself. I've never seen a situation get worse by facing it and talking about it. I'll call information and get his number."

"No, wait." Emily stood up from the table, desperate to stop Helen. "I'm not ready."

"I'll just get his number, not dial it." She marched to the phone, called information, and came up with a number for Hanson and Coltrain, but nothing for Jake Hanson or, at Emily's suggestion, J. Joe Hanson.

"His private phone is probably unlisted. I'll call the company and see if they'll give it to me."

Emily sank back into her chair. She shouldn't let Helen do this. But to hear Jake's voice again would be so wonderful. She bit her lip and grabbed the edge of the table to keep from stopping her friend.

"Yes, Jake Hanson's office please. Hmmmm, are you sure about that?" A long pause. "Do you have a number where I could reach him? He has? Thank you." Helen hung up the phone and turned around, a thoughtful expression on her face.

Emily couldn't imagine what Helen had heard. "C'mon, the suspense is killing me."

"Jake Hanson is no longer with the company. It seems he sold his shares and retired."

"Retired?" Emily echoed. "What does that mean?"

"It means I'm back, Emily."

twenty-five

The masculine voice dropped into the room like a bomb.

Emily rose and whirled around. Her knees buckled, and Jake caught her.

Jake took in her pallor and the weight she'd lost as he settled her back into her chair and knelt beside her.

Stephie came up beside him, her brow furrowed with worry as she looked at her big sister.

"Are you all right?" He cradled Emily's face in his palms. "Emily, honey, Stephie told me you didn't get any of my letters. I'm so sorry. Sid was supposed to be forwarding them."

"Jake," Emily whispered his name and shook her head as if she was trying to clear it.

"I spent the last month in the Philippines. They sent me to an island off the coast of Mindanao where the closest thing to a phone was a two-way radio. I could send a message, but I couldn't talk to anyone except the home base in Zamboanga."

Jake took one hand away from Emily to clench his fist. "Sid manufactured the whole thing."

Emily looked dazed and so pale he was afraid she'd faint. Jake wanted to carry her off where they could be alone forever, except he wanted Stephie to come. . .and Lucky, and Cowlick.

"He. . .he manufactured a. . .a typhoon?" She wasn't getting it, but he didn't care. She was here. He could touch her.

"No, he just manufactured my isolation. He picked the most primitive, remote spot in the whole disastrous place. It was awful. The destruction, the death." Jake let his fist rest on Emily's knee and lowered his forehead to rest on his hand. He knew he had to take care of her, but the tragedy haunted him. He'd been desperate to get back here. Desperate to escape all

159

that misery. Desperate to stop the hammering of his heart.

Emily—he had to think of her now, not himself. He had to find some remaining strength.

A hand rested on the top of his head and slid into his hair. A hand that could only be Emily's. Another, smaller hand, Stephie's, patted the corded knots on his shoulders.

He was home. They'd already begun taking care of him. He wanted to cry and he might have, except he was too happy. He raised his head with renewed strength. "You told me I had to learn to say no, but so many lives were at stake I couldn't. Sid had me convinced all the manpower possible was needed, but what he really wanted was me, back in harness and out of the loop."

"And Tish? Could you say no to her? Are you still engaged?" The voice was so weak, so hurt, not like his Emily's at all.

Jake hadn't thought about Tish in all this mess. The trouble had always been between him and Sid, but Emily hadn't known that.

"Engaged? I've never been engaged to her. I've only dated her when I've been in the country, and for the last few years that's only been a few weeks total. There's nothing between us. There never was. I—" Jake was suddenly aware that he had an audience. A strange woman.

He looked back into Emily's exhausted, shining eyes. "Are you all right, sweetheart?"

"I'm glad to see you, Jake. Are you here for a visit?"

Jake wasn't getting through to her. How could he say all he wanted with other people around? Emily had a hint of color in her face now. He let go of her and stood, wrapping an arm around Stephie.

"No, I'm not here for a visit."

He saw Emily's face fall and he wanted to hold her and comfort her and cry and laugh and maybe do a few dance steps, because he was so happy to be alive and in this place with the women he loved.

"I'm here to stay. I'm finished with Hanson and Coltrain." He saw her eyes narrow with doubt. Well, time would fix that. But he didn't have much time, since he was planning on marrying her this afternoon. He shouldn't have stopped to pet Lucky.

Jake looked at the woman standing with her arm resting protectively on Emily's shoulders. Not a stranger, for sure, so maybe she could babysit for a while. He extended his free hand, never letting go of Stephie. "I'm Jake. Jake Hanson. I live over the hill at the Barrett place."

"You don't say." Helen's hand came up but Jake didn't miss the sarcasm. "I'm Helen Murray. I'm Emily's nearest neighbor and best friend."

Jake got the implied threat. He took a deep breath and pressed onward. "Glad to meet you, Helen. Emily has told me a lot of good things about you."

"Emily has told me a lot about you, too." Unlike Jake's little greeting, Helen's wasn't a compliment.

Jake tried again. "I need to talk to Emily for a while. I don't suppose Stephie could go to your house for a while?"

"Not on your life." Helen crossed her arms.

Jake's eyes really met Helen's for the first time. He saw a formidable woman, one who wasn't budging.

"I'd be glad to wait outside for a few minutes though." Helen gave him a warmer smile than he deserved, considering Emily's thin shoulders and pale cheeks.

Jake squared his shoulders. It didn't matter. He'd been planning to be the perfect gentleman anyway.

"Helen, it's all right. I'll be fine with Jake."

"We'll see about that. So far things haven't been all that fine."

Jake saw humor alongside the wisdom in Helen.

Helen took Stephie's hand and led her outside. Just before the door swung shut, she turned. "Ten minutes."

The door clicked shut and Jake dragged Emily out of the chair and kissed her senseless. When he had to breathe, he said,

"I love you, Emily. I've missed you every minute, every second. I thought I'd made arrangements for you to be contacted regularly."

He kissed her again, drawing strength just from touching her. "Before I left for the Philippines, I told Sid I was selling out and staying here with you. He must have hoped he could keep me in line if he ruined things between us."

Jake looked at Emily's thin face. "He hasn't, has he? Ruined things?"

Emily reached a trembling hand to Jake's face, as if to convince herself he was real. "You love me? Do you mean it? Are you really back to stay?"

"I'm really back to stay."

Emily shook her head.

Jake nodded. "You'll start to believe me after we've been married about ten years." He pulled her into his arms again and did his best to be entirely, thoroughly, exhaustively convincing. When he came up for air, they were sitting on her couch in the living room. She was on his lap and her long hair was loose from its braid and flowing around them like living water.

"Honey, this whole mess helped me to see that I'm not indispensable. I've wanted out of my old life, but for the first time I knew where else I wanted to be. Any competent engineer can do what I do. I'm not going to have any trouble saying no from now on. Listen, I've been practicing."

Jake lowered his voice nearly an octave. "I'm sorry. You'll have to get someone else." He spoke normally. "How's that? Or this one." The tone deepened again. "I can't leave my wife. She's eight months pregnant with our tenth child." Jake pulled back so he could see her eyes. "Or is that ten months pregnant with our eighth child?"

Emily laughed, and Jake knew they were going to get through this. He'd known anyway because he planned to marry Emily if it took twenty years to convince her to say yes. But he desperately did *not* want it to take twenty years. He pulled her close.

She pushed him away. Her blue eyes met the dark brown of his. "Was that a proposal? Because if it was, it was the worst one I've ever heard."

"Oh, how many have you heard?" His mock jealousy took the last of the misery out of her eyes.

She leaned until her forehead pressed against his, closed her eyes, and whispered, "Just one."

"You will marry me, won't you?" He rested both hands on her face and lifted her chin until he could see her eyes. "You deserve so much better than me. It took me so long to realize how wonderful you are. I was so awful at first. Remember the time I—"

Emily pressed two fingers softly against his lips and silenced him. "I remember every word you've ever spoken to me, Jake. I've been thinking of nothing else for a month."

He lifted her hand from his mouth and kissed each fingertip. "Oh, sweetheart, I'm sorry, so terribly sorry you've been so unhappy."

"Now that you're back"—her neat little speech faltered— "there's nothing left to be sorry for."

"You've never said you'll marry me, but you don't have to. We're already married in our hearts. I know that because I was only half alive without you, and I only have to look at you to see you feel the same. We share one heart, one soul. We're already married in the best sense of the word."

Emily blinked. "I've thought the same thing. But I thought I was feeling it alone."

"It took some doing for me to get past my job, my mother's desertion, and my father's neglect. But I was in love and committed to you for life from the moment"—he smiled—"I fell on top of you. You can say anything you want, it's only words. We are married. When do you want to do the paperwork?"

Emily laughed again.

"So, do you want a big ceremony, the white dress and the flowers? We can do anything you want."

"No big ceremony. I just want you. I love you, Jake."

Jake raised his eyes to hers as she spoke the words he longed to hear. "How could I have been such a fool to leave before we'd said all the important things to each other?"

"When you left, you weren't sure you cared about me."

"I loved you," Jake said sternly.

"You had doubts. So did I. We needed this time. Now we're both ready, we're both sure. That's so easy to say now that you're here." She added, "I want to do the paperwork just as soon as possible."

He chuckled. "Good. I know a few people and I pulled a few strings and managed to get this marriage license." Jake pulled it out of his pocket.

Her eyes widened. "Don't I need to be there to get this?"

"Sign it. I'm a notary public. I brought my stamp." He produced a stamp from the same pocket.

Emily laughed. "So, you're saying if I sign this we're married? I've never heard of this before. It sounds like a great system."

"Well, someone should speak some vows, I suppose. But the paperwork is what makes it legal. We're married enough for me."

Jake kissed her.

"Well, you're not married enough for me. So knock it off."

Emily jumped out of Jake's lap and Jake sagged back against the couch. He looked at the neighborhood guard dog. "The fair Helen has returned."

"I gave you twenty minutes instead of ten. So you should be thanking me."

"Yeah, thanks a lot." There wasn't a single teeny-tiny iota of thankfulness in him.

Helen took the paper out of Emily's hand. "This isn't legal."

Emily had the grace to blush. Jake had the grace not to kill Helen. "Yes, Helen, it is."

Helen fastened such a stern look on him it was all he could do to not sit up straight and revert to a schoolboy. "You can't get a marriage license without both of you going to the courthouse."

"I've been on the phone since I got back into a place my cell would work." He glared at Emily. "Including I tried to call you a thousand times from airports on my way back from the Philippines. You're getting an answering machine and cell phone that you will keep turned on at all times."

"B–But those are modern conveniences."

"So?"

"Pioneers didn't have them."

Jake narrowed his eyes.

"And besides, cell phones don't work out here."

"I found that out. But they worked fine in Tokyo and LA and Chicago and Rapid City."

"Is that how you get home from the Philippines?"

"Yes. Why didn't you answer the phone?"

"I was busy."

Jake sighed and turned back to Helen. "I had the marriage license faxed to me in my Chicago office."

"Emily has to be there."

"Not if the county judge comes to the wedding and verifies everything."

"You know the county judge?" Helen arched one brow doubtfully.

"No, but I know a guy who knows a guy who does." Jake glanced at his watch. "But he's just a backup. I want a pastor to bless our marriage. If not now, then soon. But we're getting married today and that's that."

Helen glared. "Emily never had a chance resisting you, did she?"

Jake wanted to be insulted, but a spark in Helen's eye made him realize it might be the very first compliment the old harpy had given him. "I never had a chance with her either."

Helen looked at Emily. Jake knew Helen could see the torment gone from Emily's expression and the color back in her cheeks. Helen wouldn't try to stop Emily from marrying him, not that he'd let her.

"Do you want to marry him, honey?"

Emily nodded. "Oh, yes."

Jake smiled and she took a step toward him.

Helen's voice stopped her. "I suppose you want to marry him right now?"

Emily's eyes flashed, and Jake remembered the woman who had fought for her elm tree and chopped a load of wood before he was awake in the morning and spent hours up to her neck in the mud to save a cow. Despite the pain he'd caused her, she still had spirit.

"Well, Helen, either I can marry him right now or you can sign this license where it says 'witness' and take Stephie and leave us alone. Show her your stamp, Jake."

Helen laughed. "No, the stamp won't be necessary. How about if we do all three? Marriage first, signature second, taking Stephie third."

Emily blushed.

Helen said, "I think I can track down Pastor Lewis, and your dirty T-shirt isn't quite a wedding dress."

"Well, Jake, say something." Emily looked at him as if daring him to back out.

Like there was a chance in the world he'd let her escape.

He fired off a few orders of his own. "Emily, go get a dress on. Helen, call the pastor." He tugged on the lapel of his chambray shirt. "I'm going home to put a suit on. I'll be ready in ten minutes."

He went to Emily under Helen's watchful eye, and leaned close to her ear. "In our wedding, I had you pictured wearing blue jeans and work boots."

With shining eyes, she closed one fist over the collar of his blue work shirt. "I never pictured a wedding for us."

"I'll pick out a dress and get the shower started." Helen headed down the hall. Gone but not forgotten.

Emily called after her. "I want to wear my white sundress!"

Helen nodded.

"The sundress won't take ten minutes to put on, hotshot."

Jake grabbed her wrist for old time's sake. It was completely different than in the early days.

Emily laughed. "I had your electricity disconnected. Let's call and get it turned back on while we're at the church."

Jake nodded. "It's Saturday, so they won't get to it until Monday. We can stay here until they get it done."

"So, you're going to do it? Go all modern?"

"Yes, you win. . .again. . .like always."

"When have I ever won with you? I've been taking orders since we met." Emily shook him by the lapels.

"Are you kidding? I can't remember your being the least bit obedient."

Emily laughed. "You know I haven't laughed once since you left. I'm so glad you're back. I want you to know. . ." She hesitated.

"What? You can tell me anything."

"I want you to know I'm yours, Jake. This last month I found out where I am doesn't matter. I just have to be with you. So if things don't work out for you here, I'll follow you anywhere."

Jake hugged her until her feet lifted off the floor. "I've found out a lot, too. I found out Sid was embezzling. I found out my distrust of people came about because I was hanging around with the wrong ones. I'd trust you with my life. After ten minutes with Helen, ten lo-o-ng minutes"—Emily laughed again as Jake set her on her feet—"I'd trust her, too. I've lived my whole life either working myself to death in horrible conditions or with limo drivers and four-star restaurants. I didn't even know how real people lived. I wanted so badly to escape that life and get back to nature that I thought I had to give up everything—electricity, phones, mail, people."

"All you ever had to do was stop and look around. There are real people everywhere, including among the rich. How rich are you anyway?"

"Well, I was rich before I sold Hanson and Coltrain."

"Did that hurt you financially to do that?"

For a moment her interest almost resurrected his old, distrustful self. "Would it matter if it did?"

Emily's eyes narrowed. "I just hated to think of your giving up a fortune for me. It seems like the kind of thing you might regret later. I really ought to pound you for asking if it mattered, hotshot."

He let go of distrust for the last time. "Anyway, I was rich then, but now I'm *really* rich."

"Really rich?"

"Oh, man."

"We don't have to spend it, do we, honey? I think too much wealth kind of wrecks people."

"No, we don't. And I like 'honey' better than 'hotshot.'"

"Oh, you do not!"

Jake laughed and swung her around in his arms. Her long hair flew out and his heart nearly exploded when he thought of all of this strength and beauty being his. "We can fix the Barrett place up all you want. Or would you rather live here? This would make a wonderful home." He held her with her feet dangling off the floor.

"I've always loved the Barrett. . .excuse me, I mean the Hanson place."

Jake nodded his approval. "I like the sound of that."

Emily looked into his eyes. "When I woke up this morning, my life stretched in front of me like a thousand miles of un-inhabited Black Hills. I never expected to be happy again. I've always believed happiness came from inside. But you took it with you when you left. I'm almost scared to love you so much."

Jake saw the tears swimming in her blue eyes and knew the sting of his own. Yes, with Emily he was definitely going to live forever. Laughing and crying. Saying no and saying yes, yes, yes. Leaving his stress behind just by holding her in his arms.

"I didn't believe love existed until I met you. I don't think I've ever been given true love before. Not from my mother or father. Not from the women I dated. But one single day with you and my whole world turned around. And Stephie. She's so precious. I fell in love with her the minute she came into your kitchen and said, 'Hi, Jake,' after all our worrying about her finding out about me.

"And God. You helped me find enough peace so I could open myself to Him again. You're a gift to me, straight from a loving God. I only hope I can be worthy of that gift and make you and Stephie as happy as you've made me."

Emily had been holding him tight as he talked. He looked into her eyes and saw his love reflected back. "You want to make me happy?"

Jake nodded.

She kissed his lips as softly as a breath of air. "Then go away."

His eyebrows arched with surprise.

"And get a suit on and get back here."

Jake kissed her hard, then turned and ran.

For the very first time in his life he was running toward something—a family, love, faith.

At last, he was running toward home.

epilogue

The judge showed up and had to produce some ID to convince Helen he was the real thing. It helped that Pastor Lewis was his fishing buddy.

Emily was embarrassed, but all things considered, it was probably best that Helen was in charge of this slapdash ceremony.

The word got out about the wedding even before they got to the church. Ladies with casserole dishes were at work in the church kitchen. The pastor's wife had driven into Hot Springs and grabbed an armload of roses in every color they had at the local discount store. She'd even come up with a wedding cake of sorts. It wasn't tiered with a bride and groom on top, but it was a sheet cake, pretty, dotted with flowers.

Helen played the organ as she did every week. Her music was as perfect as if she'd talked for hours with Emily about which songs would be best.

The vows were spoken. They sang a hymn together and ate a feast and were still home in time for chores and a honeymoon in Emily's dream house, which was nearly perfectly restored by Jake, a top-notch carpenter who was no longer a clueless cowboy.

A Letter To Our Readers

Dear Reader:

In order that we might better contribute to your reading enjoyment, we would appreciate your taking a few minutes to respond to the following questions. We welcome your comments and read each form and letter we receive. When completed, please return to the following:

Fiction Editor
Heartsong Presents
PO Box 719
Uhrichsville, Ohio 44683

1. Did you enjoy reading *Clueless Cowboy* by Mary Connealy?
   ❑ Very much! I would like to see more books by this author!
   ❑ Moderately. I would have enjoyed it more if

   _____

   _____

   _____

2. Are you a member of **Heartsong Presents**? ❑ Yes ❑ No
   If no, where did you purchase this book? _____

   _____

3. How would you rate, on a scale from 1 (poor) to 5 (superior),
   the cover design? _____

4. On a scale from 1 (poor) to 10 (superior), please rate the
   following elements.

   ____ Heroine   ____ Plot
   ____ Hero   ____ Inspirational theme
   ____ Setting   ____ Secondary characters

5. These characters were special because? _____

_____

_____

6. How has this book inspired your life? _____

_____

_____

7. What settings would you like to see covered in future
   Heartsong Presents books? _____

_____

_____

8. What are some inspirational themes you would like to see
   treated in future books? _____

_____

_____

9. Would you be interested in reading other **Heartsong
   Presents** titles? ❏ Yes   ❏ No

10. Please check your age range:

    ❏ Under 18   ❏ 18-24

    ❏ 25-34   ❏ 35-45

    ❏ 46-55   ❏ Over 55

Name _____

Occupation _____

Address _____

City, State, Zip _____

MARY CONNEALY

Schoolmarm Grace Calhoun
has her work cut out for her
with the Reeves boys—five
malicious monsters of mayhem
who are making her life
miserable. Things couldn't get
any worse. . .or could they?

Historical, paperback, 288 pages, $5^{3}/_{16}$" x 8"

_____

Please send me _____ copies of *Calico Canyon*. I am enclosing $10.97 for each.
(Please add $4.00 to cover postage and handling per order. OH add 7% tax.
If outside the U.S. please call 740-922-7280 for shipping charges.)

Name_____

Address _____

City, State, Zip _____

To place a credit card order, call 1-740-922-7280.
Send to: Heartsong Presents Readers' Service, PO Box 721, Uhrichsville, OH 44683

Heart♥ong

Any 12
Heartsong
Presents titles
for only
$27.00*

CONTEMPORARY ROMANCE IS CHEAPER BY THE DOZEN!

Buy any assortment of twelve *Heartsong Presents* titles and save 25% off the already discounted price of $2.97 each!

*plus $4.00 shipping and handling per order and sales tax where applicable. If outside the U.S. please call 740-922-7280 for shipping charges.

HEARTSONG PRESENTS TITLES AVAILABLE NOW:

(If ordering from this page, please remember to include it with the order form.)

HEARTSONG
PRESENTS

If you love Christian romance...

$10.⁹⁹

You'll love Heartsong Presents' inspiring and faith-filled romances by today's very best Christian authors...Wanda E. Brunstetter, Mary Connealy, Susan Page Davis, Cathy Marie Hake, and Joyce Livingston, to mention a few!

When you join Heartsong Presents, you'll enjoy four brand-new, mass market, 176-page books—two contemporary and two historical—that will build you up in your faith when you discover God's role in every relationship you read about!

Mass Market 176 Pages

Imagine...four new romances every four weeks—with men and women like you who long to meet the one God has chosen as the love of their lives...all for the low price of $10.99 postpaid.

To join, simply visit www.heartsong presents.com or complete the coupon below and mail it to the address provided.

- -

YES! Sign me up for Heartsong!

NEW MEMBERSHIPS WILL BE SHIPPED IMMEDIATELY!
Send no money now. We'll bill you only $10.99 postpaid with your first shipment of four books. Or for faster action, call 1-740-922-7280.

NAME _____

ADDRESS_____

CITY_____ STATE _____ ZIP _____

MAIL TO: HEARTSONG PRESENTS, P.O. Box 721, Uhrichsville, Ohio 44683
or sign up at **WWW.HEARTSONGPRESENTS.COM**